Fugitive of Sins

ROZ POTGIETER

Contents

CHAPTER 1
ARRIVAL

The heavy iron gates of Steelvale Maximum Security Prison creaked open, their metallic groan reverberating through the cold night air. Marco Carrera, notorious across the nation as the 'Designer Killer,' shuffled forward in shackles, his eyes narrowing against the floodlights' harsh glare. The guards flanking him were stone-faced, their hands resting on the butts of their holstered weapons as if any moment might require them to put down the monster they escorted.

Marco felt their tension, but it didn't faze him. His mind was elsewhere, lost in the cold calculations that had defined his every move. Nine women, nine perfect executions, all designed with the precision of an artist sculpting his masterpiece. And now, his final canvas would be the execution chamber, where the state would end his life with the same sterile efficiency he had once reserved for his victims.

He barely registered the intake procedures as he was led through the labyrinth of corridors. Fingerprinting, photographs and the exchange of his tailored suit for the dull orange of a prison jumpsuit were mere formalities, insignificant in the grand scheme. His mind was fixed on what lay ahead: death by lethal injection.

Steelvale, a high-security correctional facility with severe restrictions, was known for its rigid control, harsh conditions, and relentless discipline. It was born out of necessity—a fortress designed by the Federal Bureau of Prisons to contain the most dangerous, volatile and high-profile criminals. These were not just ordinary prisoners; they were individuals capable of extreme violence, not only toward others but also toward themselves.

The design of Steelvale reflected the nature of its inhabitants. Each prisoner was confined to a solitary cell for most of the day. Surveillance was relentless—24-hour supervision with an intensely high staff-to-inmate ratio ensured no move went unnoticed. In the chilly, silent confines of Steelvale, time seemed to stand still, leaving the prisoners to confront the stark reality of their existence.

But Marco was not a man who feared death. He had always known that his brilliance would draw attention, that the world would either revere or destroy him. As the final metal door clanged shut behind him, sealing him into the small, cold cell that would be his home until his execution, he felt nothing but a detached curiosity about the process. He had studied death so closely—now he would experience it.

The cell was bleak, a reinforced-concrete box with a narrow bunk, a stainless-steel toilet, and a small, barred window that let in a fragment of the night sky. Marco glanced at the bunk, then to the window, and finally the door. He smiled murkily. The prison's efforts to contain and break him were laughable. They didn't realize that the confines of his mind were far more impenetrable than any cell.

*   *   *

Days, weeks, and months passed in a blur of monotony. His meals were slipped through the bars in the door, lights flickered off and on with the mechanical precision of the prison's daily routine, and guards spoke to him only in clipped, detached tones. Marco relished the silence, using it to retreat into his thoughts, into the memories of his 'work.'

One evening, just as the lights dimmed for the night, there was a change in the routine. The rattle of a door opening down the hall caught Marco's attention. He listened, his senses sharpening. Footsteps—he counted four distinct pairs—echoed down the corridor, drawing closer to his cell. The steps stopped at the cell directly across from his.

Marco leaned back on his bunk, staring at the ceiling as the cell door across from him clanged shut. He could hear the guards muttering, though he couldn't make out the words. What mattered was that something had disrupted the prison's dull rhythm. Someone new had arrived.

The next morning, as the guards made their rounds, Marco got his first look at the newcomer. He was broad and sturdily built, and his face seemed chiselled from stone. His dark, wavy hair was cropped close. Marco immediately recognized a hardness in his eyes—a cold, calculating gaze that was all too familiar.

Marco's curiosity was piqued, but he kept his expression neutral as he watched the man through the bars. The newcomer's gaze flicked to him, and for a fleeting instant, their eyes locked. Marco expected the man to look away, as most did when confronted with the infamous Designer Killer. But he didn't. Instead, a slow, knowing smile spread across his face.

Marco's mind raced, dissecting that look, that smile. Something was unsettling about it—something that hinted at a connection, a familiarity. But Marco was certain he had never seen this man before. So why did it feel like the newcomer knew him?

As the day dragged on, Marco couldn't shake the feeling that the new inmate was watching him. Every time he glanced across the hall, he found the man's eyes fixed on him, that same unsettling smile tugging at the corners of his lips.

In the evening, as Marco lay on his bunk, staring at the ceiling, he heard a voice—a low, mocking whisper that drifted across the corridor.

'They say the master always meets his match, don't they?'

Marco sat up, his heart pounding for the first time in months. He turned toward the source of the voice, his eyes narrowing as he met the man's gaze.

'Who are you?' he demanded, his voice icy.

Marco had always been in control, consistently one step ahead of everyone around him. But now, for the first time, he felt a faint sense of uncertainty.

'Don't look so surprised,' the man continued, his voice dripping with malice. 'Did you think you were the only one who knew how to play the game?'

Marco's mind raced as he tried to place the man's face, his voice, anything that might give a clue to his identity. But nothing came. Whoever this man was, he was a complete enigma, and that unsettled Marco more than anything else.

The man leaned closer to the bars, his voice dropping again to a conspiratorial whisper. 'You and I, Marco... we're going to have some fun together. But first, let's see if you can figure out who I am before it's too late. For now, you can call me X.' With that, he broke into hysterical laughter.

Marco clenched his fists. Who was this man? And what did he want?

When the lights dimmed and the prison settled into its nightly stillness, Marco lay awake, his mind whirling with questions. For the first time since his arrest, he felt he wasn't in control. There was a new player in the game.

And that player was right across the hall, watching his every move.

As the night stretched on, Marco realized with a sinking feeling that he was no longer the hunter. He was the prey. And whoever this man was, he wasn't just here to watch Marco die—he was here to make him suffer first.

Marco closed his eyes, trying to regain his composure. But as sleep eluded him and the man's words echoed in his mind, he knew one thing for certain: the game wasn't over. It had only just begun.

Just when Marco thought it was safe to sleep, a faint, rasping whisper seeped through the bars of his cell like an insidious fog.

'How many, Marco?' the voice began, barely audible but cutting through the silence like a blade. 'Do you even remember their faces? Or have they blurred into the same wide-eyed stares?'

Marco's jaw locked, his fists clenching so hard that his nails bit into his palms. He refused to rise to it.

'Silence isn't absolution, you know. It's just cowardice,' X continued. 'Now it all makes sense to me. I thought you were too weak to act alone. You relied heavily on your accomplices, didn't you? The ones in your head. You are more fucked up than I ever imagined.'

X let out a hissing breath. 'Surly thinks you're strong enough for this, right?' he sneered. 'But he's wrong. He's the weak link, Marco. He's the one dragging you down.'

Marco's eyes flew open, his breath hitching. The mention of Surly was like a slap to the face. Surly, the part of him that had always been the voice of reason, the only tether keeping him from slipping entirely into madness. How did X know about Surly? No one knew about Surly.

The whispers escalated to laughter, harsh and jagged. 'Oh, I know all about your little compartmentalized tricks. Surly, the negotiator. The one who tries to make sense of the carnage. Pathetic. Let me tell you something, Marco: guilt isn't a leash. It's a noose. And Surly's been tightening it around your neck this whole time.'

Marco shot up from his bunk, his hands gripping the cold bars of his cell. 'Shut up,' he growled, his voice raw and trembling. 'You don't know me. You don't know a damn thing about me.'

'Oh, but I do,' X taunted, his voice rising, sharp and condescending. 'You think the guards keep your secrets? Steelvale's walls have ears, Marco. Every muttered confession—every whimper in the dark. I've heard it all. And Surly?' He spat the name like poison. 'He's ashamed of you. Nine women, Marco. Innocent. Helpless. Their screams echo louder in your head than my whispers ever could.'

Marco staggered back as though the words had physically struck him. His breathing was ragged, his heart pounding so loudly he thought it might burst.

X leaned closer to the bars of his cell, his face partially illuminated by the dim, flickering light from the corridor. His lips curled into a cruel grin. The darkness behind his eyes seemed endless as he relentlessly gnawed at Marco's psyche like a parasite.

'Do you hear them, Marco? Do you hear their cries for mercy? Or does Surly's pathetic guilt drown them out?'

'Leave him out of this,' Marco hissed, his voice cracking. 'This is between you and me.'

X's laugh echoed through the cellblock. 'There is no 'you and me,' Carrera. There's only me and your crumbling mind. And I've decided Surly's the first to go.'

* * *

The corridor's dim light cast long shadows on the unforgiving concrete walls. The other inmates, including X, were sound asleep. The only noise was the faint drip of water from a pipe overhead, creating an eerie rhythm in the silence. Marco sat on the edge of his bunk, his elbows on his knees and his hands clasped as though holding something fragile. His knuckles weren't white with tension—they were red, smeared with dried blood. His head was lowered, his face hidden, but the darkness in the room felt alive with another presence.

'Marco, we need to talk,' Surly said, his voice low and trembling. He wasn't flesh and blood—never had been. He was more a flicker of conscience, a shimmer of light shaped by guilt and memory. A spectral glint of who Marco used to be.

Marco didn't look up. 'Talk about what?'

'About what you've done. What *we've* done. I can't keep... I can't keep being part of this.'

Marco's mouth stretched into a sardonic smile. 'You've always been here, Surly. You don't get to pick and choose now. That's not how this works.'

Surly's voice grew louder in Marco's head. 'Look around, Marco! Look where we are. Look what you've become! You don't even try to justify it anymore. The blood, the screams, the faces of the people you've killed. They haunt me. Don't they haunt you?'

Marco finally raised his head, his piercing eyes locking onto the bare cell wall. 'No. They don't. And if they haunt you, that's your problem. You were always the weak one. The one whining about right and wrong. Rip gets it. He knows what it takes to survive.'

At the mention of Rip, Surly's voice lowered. 'Rip doesn't survive.

Rip *destroys*. Rip revels in the chaos while you... you just let him. You let him dictate who you are. And me? I've just been sanctioning it all. I'm complicit. That's on me.'

Marco leaned back against the wall, his smile fading. 'You sound tired. You know what happens to the tired, don't you? They give up. They fade away. Maybe that's for the best.'

Surly hesitated. 'You think I haven't thought about it? Leaving you, leaving this... mess? I have. But I stayed because I hoped, Marco. I hoped that maybe, just maybe, there was something left of you worth saving. But now? I don't know.'

'Spare me the drama,' Marco snapped. 'If you want to go, go. You've been nothing but a weight around my neck anyway. Always second-guessing, always preaching.'

Surly's voice broke. 'Do you even hear yourself? Do you even care? You weren't always like this. I remember when we debated the smallest things—what was fair and what wasn't. Now, you don't even flinch when Rip takes control and leaves bodies in our wake. I can't do it anymore.'

'Then don't,' Marco said, standing. His shadow stretched across the cell. 'But don't think for a second that you're better than me. You're part of me, Surly. You always will be. You've got just as much blood on your hands as I do.'

Surly's voice was barely a whisper. 'Maybe. But I'm done with it. Done with you.'

Marco gave a cold, empty laugh. 'We'll see about that. You don't get to walk away.'

Surly's form wavered, his edges dissolving into the darkness of Marco's mind. 'I'm already gone, Marco. You just don't know it yet.'

For a moment, the cell was silent again, broken only by the faint dripping of water. Marco stood alone, his eyes held secrets his face

refused to show. But deep in the shadows, another presence stirred;
a murkier, more menacing figure.

Rip.

'Don't worry,' Rip growled, his voice like gravel. 'He'll be back.
They always come back. But even if he doesn't... we don't need him.
Do we, Marco?'

Marco flashed a grin that knew too much, his voice icy. 'No, we
don't.'

* * *

The following day, Marco paced the perimeter of the yard, which
was—unusually—empty of other inmates. His thoughts spun like
a whirlwind, colliding and scattering faster than he could catch
them. Then, out of nowhere, he heard the echo of heavy, deliberate
footsteps, cutting through the quiet. Immediately, Marco turned,
heart pounding, and there he was.

X.

That now all-too-familiar face was moving toward Marco with
a slow, almost lazy stride, his broad, muscular frame imposing, his
gaze as sharp and unyielding as steel. Marco tensed, every muscle
in his body on edge. *Jeezus, this fuck is relentless*, Marco thought,
not taking his eyes off X. Facing him across the prison bars had
been unsettling enough, but in the open yard without any barriers
between them? The vulnerability was unnerving, and Marco was
getting tired of it.

As X came closer, the guards looked on, their faces unreadable,
doing nothing to intervene. X stopped a few feet away, his eyes
narrowing with a strange, predatory gleam, his mouth twitched
with quiet triumph. Marco's instincts screamed at him to move,

but he held his ground, refusing to show fear.

Still there was no intervention from the guards, who watched closely but said nothing. X's grin widened as he took another step toward Marco.

'Marco,' he finally said, low and laced with an unsettling calm. 'At last, we stand face to face – no cold metal between us.'

Marco didn't reply. His instincts were on high alert. He searched for any hint of X's intentions on his face, but X's expression was inscrutable. A moment passed, silent but charged, before X leaned in, his voice barely above a whisper, eyes gleaming with dark, twisted amusement.

'It's strange, isn't it?' he asked. 'How fate brings people together in the most unexpected places. Some might call it coincidence... but I know better.'

The words slithered through Marco's mind like a venomous snake, coiling tight. His pulse quickened, but he fought to keep his voice steady. 'Who are you?' he demanded, his tone firm. 'What do you want?'

X's smirk widened into a chilling grin. 'Who I am doesn't matter. What I want, Marco, is you. All of you.' His voice dropped, dripping with menace. 'And I won't rest until I see you broken.'

Marco swallowed, willing himself not to react, but he could feel his resolve wavering under X's gaze. There was a darkness in this man, a hollow rage that twisted his words with frightening conviction. Marco had been threatened before, but X was different. He seemed like someone who enjoyed watching fear take root in others, someone who fed on suffering, and this was no idle threat.

'Think you're untouchable?' Marco retorted, defiant. 'You don't know who you're dealing with.'

X's grin slipped, twisting into something more challenging, a cold determination. 'Oh, I know exactly who I'm dealing with,' he hissed. 'A monster, a killer. And you're right, monsters are dangerous.' He took a step closer, his face inches from Marco's. 'But even monsters bleed.'

For a tense moment, neither of them moved, their standoff filling the heavy air with an electric charge. Marco could feel X's breath, hot and steady, a reminder of just how close this danger truly was. Finally, with a sneer, X leaned back.

'The best is yet to come, Marco,' he murmured. 'I'm going to enjoy tearing down whatever's left of you. You'll wish you'd never laid eyes on me.'

* * *

A few days later, the air hung heavy, slick with sweat, cigarette smoke, and the silent tension that made men uneasy, all baking under the relentless sun. The yard was the only place where Marco could see Eddie.

Eddie—cunning, ruthless, and as sharp as Marco himself. Stocky and weathered, with curly blonde hair that did little to soften the menace in his eyes, he had connections, leverage, and, above all, a seething grudge against the system that had betrayed him. It was Eddie whom Marco confided in after killing Ava, his first victim. And it was Eddie who led him to Noctis. The cabal was a force of whispered legends, feared yet unseen, shaping destinies from the shadows. They were more than a secret society; they were the architects of power.

With Eddie at his side, escape was a possibility. Especially if Noctis was involved.

Marco walked across the cracked concrete with a neutral

expression, hands tucked in his pockets, his sharp green eyes scanning the usual clusters of inmates. Every muscle in his body was coiled tight, pulse drumming with quiet urgency. Every step was measured. Since X's arrival, he had spent days mapping this place out—the blind spots, the guard rotations, the routines of the men around him.

Across the yard, Eddie leaned against the rusted fence, his arms crossed like he didn't have a care in the world. The brim of a prison-issued cap shaded his dark eyes. To anyone else, he was just another con, another lifer with no future. But Marco knew better. Eddie arrived here before him. Weeks before. Marco had never questioned it out loud, but the thought gnawed at him. Was Eddie planted? Had he known Marco was coming?

Marco strolled over, stopping just beside him, their eyes barely meeting.

'You look like shit,' Marco muttered.

Eddie smirked. 'And yet, I still outshine you.'

Marco snorted, leaning against the fence beside him. His voice dropped low. 'Tell me the truth. Who put you here?'

Eddie exhaled, rubbing his jaw like he was deciding how much to say. Finally, he leaned in slightly, voice barely above a whisper.

'You know who.'

Marco felt the weight of it settle on his chest. He had always known Noctis were watching, pulling strings from the shadows. But this? Planting Eddie inside before Marco even arrived? It meant one thing.

Something big was going down.

Eddie tilted his head slightly. 'Not everyone gets this kind of help, Marco. Ever wonder why Noctis gives a damn about you?'

This sent a chill through Marco's veins. Whatever was going on behind his eyes, he wasn't sharing it. 'I don't ask questions when

I like the answers.'

Eddie chuckled. 'Smart. But you ever wonder why I'm here?'

Marco finally turned his head slightly, his eyes narrowing. 'You saying I should?'

'I'm saying everything in this place is a move on the board. Me being here? Not an accident. You being here? Not an accident.' Eddie's voice was calm, but there was an edge to it. A dangerous one.

Marco clenched his jaw. 'How long have you been on their payroll?' he asked, keeping his voice casual despite the thunder flickering beneath his ribs.

Eddie chuckled. 'Long enough to make myself disappear.'

And that part was true. No records. No fingerprints. No history. Eddie—if that was even his real name—didn't exist. Noctis had wiped him clean.

'Why me?' Marco asked.

Eddie turned his head slightly, studying him. 'Because you're it, Marco. The one they've been waiting for. You've got what they need—the right instincts, the right mindset. And most importantly—' Eddie paused, his voice turning razor-sharp— 'you don't hesitate.'

Marco stared at him, his pulse now slow and steady. 'They want me to officially join the family?'

Smirking with superiority, Eddie responded. 'The *family* doesn't exist. Noctis isn't some street gang or two-bit syndicate. You don't join it, Marco. You become part of it. A cog in a machine bigger than anything you can imagine.'

Marco exhaled, rolling his shoulders. 'And you? What's your part in this?'

'Let's just say I clear the path for men like you.'

Marco shifted his stance. 'How tight are the rotations?'

'Loose enough,' Eddie said. 'But the real issue is the east gate.'

Marco nodded. He had been watching it too.

'We need leverage,' Eddie continued. 'Something to make them look somewhere else.'

'Or someone,' Marco murmured.

Eddie's lips twitched. 'Now you're thinking like them. Thinking like *him.*'

Marco knew who Eddie meant. The shadow behind every throne, the architect of silence, a man whose name was never spoken—only felt, like a sudden drop in temperature. No one had ever seen his face. But word had it his eyes were like polished obsidian. His voice curved around your spine—low, silken, and cold as a blade— slipping through hidden speakers, crackling through encrypted calls, echoing from the mouths of those he'd already broken. He didn't need to raise his hand to make the world kneel. His presence was a ripple in the air, a static hum before the storm. Orders came, empires fell, and people vanished—always without warning or question. To defy him was to become a ghost. To serve him was to become his shadow. They called him many names—The Phantom, The Architect, The Voice. No one knew if he kept secrets in—or let monsters out. He was the head of Noctis. The unseen hand.

Marco exhaled, the pieces clicking into place. 'So, what? I pass your little test, and I get my golden ticket?'

Eddie let out a low laugh. 'You already passed. The second you put that knife in Sleazy Al's neck without blinking.'

Marco said nothing. The memory of his trial to be accepted into Noctis had faded into a dull hum, an act as easy as breathing. Eddie had been there afterward and had listened as Marco confessed—not in guilt, but in clarity. Killing dozens of victims, hunting them through a labyrinth... It had felt right.

'You were made for this,' Eddie continued. 'That's why you're in this shithole. Not because of a bad break, not because of a mistake. Because they want you.'

Marco let the words settle before he spoke again. 'And what if I don't want them?'

Eddie smiled, slow and knowing. 'Then you wouldn't be standing here talking to me.'

A whistle blew from the guard tower. Rotation shift. Two minutes until fresh eyes were on them. During their brief freedom, Marco wondered—who the hell was Eddie, really? And just how deep had Noctis pulled him in? Because two things were certain. There was no such thing as coincidence. And there was no way out.

Marco took a step back. 'This plan—how long we talking?'

Eddie shrugged. 'Six months. Maybe a year. Depends on how quickly we can set the pieces.'

Marco offered a lopsided grin, all mockery and malice. 'Patience isn't my strong suit.'

Eddie grinned back at him. 'Good thing it's mine.'

The guards started herding them inside. As Marco strode away, his mind burned with possibilities.

Noctis had put him here instead of Menard Correctional Center. Now, things were becoming clearer. And soon enough, they'd get him out.

And after that? The real work would begin.

The fuse is lit…

CHAPTER 2
THE MYSTERY X

Unspoken urgency pressed against the office walls. Warden Caleb Flannery, a formidable man in his fifties, had the kind of authority that weighed on a person, leaving no room for negotiation. His demeanour was unyielding. He sat behind a massive mahogany desk, his fingers laced together, eyes locked onto the man across from him.

X sat in a chair designed to be uncomfortable, his posture deceptively relaxed. He had spent years studying human behaviour, perfecting the art of control. But here, in the heart of Steelvale, control belonged to Flannery.

Flannery leaned forward, exhaling slowly. 'How are things going with Carrera?'

X tilted his head. 'Yeah, coming along well. I'm on target. There's some fear, although he likes to try and hide it.'

A smirk ghosted across Flannery's face. 'You're a clever man, Doctor. You know exactly what we need.' He tapped his fingers on the desk. 'Marco. The 'Designer Killer.' He's a narcissist, a manipulator, and worse—he's enjoying this. Enjoying the notoriety, the fear. He thinks he's untouchable. We need to strip him of that illusion.'

'So, you and the system believe I'm the man for that job?'

Flannery nodded. 'You're not just a forensic psychiatrist—you're a predator of the mind. Marco can con the guards, the inmates, the press... but he can't con you.' He paused, eyes darkening. 'He will break. He just doesn't know it yet.'

X held the warden's gaze. 'What exactly does breaking him entail?'

With slow, deliberate movements, Flannery stood, stepping around his desk. 'Marco thrives on power. He crafts his own narrative, bends reality to fit his design. You're going to unmake him. Piece by piece. Thought by thought.' He placed both hands on the desk, leaning in. 'You will be his shadow, his tormentor, his undoing.'

X remained still, absorbing every word. 'And his alter egos?'

Flannery's eyes narrowed. 'They're the key. Marco hides behind them, shifts between them like a man slipping through shadows. Break them, and you break him.'

'I've already dismantled the weaker of the two,' X said, his lips slightly curled.

For a long moment, Flannery studied him, before nodding. 'Good. But the stronger one... that's where the real battle begins. That's where you need to be relentless.'

'And when he's broken?'

Flannery's teeth clenched behind a tight-lipped glare. 'Then we get what we need.'

X exhaled, his mind already constructing the psychological scaffolding that would bring Marco to his knees. 'I'm just curious about one thing. Why me, specifically? There must have been other candidates.'

Whatever was going on behind Flannery's eyes, he wasn't sharing it. 'Because you understand loss, Doctor. More than most.'

X met the warden's gaze without flinching. 'I didn't sign up for this easily. Craig had to push hard to get me on board. The idea of being locked up with these psychopaths, breathing the same air as them, isn't exactly appealing.' He let the words settle before adding, 'But my conscience won out. I owed it to my profession—to the Champaign PD—to break Carrera.' His voice dipped. 'It's been hell for my parents. When can I see them?'

Flannery studied him, pokerfaced. 'Craig went to war for you. He trusts you. And let's just say... I have my own reasons for knowing you're the only one who can do this.' He straightened. 'I'll arrange the visit.'

'Appreciate that,' X said, his voice even. 'When do I get full access to his files?'

'Soon. In a few weeks, we're pulling you out of Steelvale—temporarily. An unexpected transfer. You'll spend time with Craig in Champaign to go through everything.'

A beat of silence passed between them, electric with implication. X didn't press. That answer would come in time. Instead, he leaned forward, a slow, knowing smile forming on his lips. 'Then let's finish this.'

As the door closed behind him, the warden sat back in his chair. The shadows seemed to grow in the dim light, filling the room with an oppressive weight. And in the silence, a single thought lingered: would breaking Marco be enough to stop him.

* * *

The prison yard was a stark contrast to the suffocating confines of the cells, but no less hostile. The sun was merciless, baking the cracked concrete and casting long, jagged shadows. Marco usually found the yard his only place of solace, a brief escape from the stifling darkness of his cell. But today, the air felt charged with an unshakable sense of danger. He could feel something—a presence, a gaze, stalking him in silence.

Marco's muscles tensed as he stepped into the yard, the oppressive weight of eyes on him from every corner. Steelvale's guards leaned lazily against the fences, their expressions indifferent. They wouldn't intervene. Not here.

X was waiting. He stood among a cluster of inmates, his presence commanding yet eerily understated. When Marco approached, the crowd parted, like predators retreating to give the alpha space.

'How are you holding up, Marco?' X asked, his tone dripping with mock concern. 'Surly still whispering sweet nothings in your ear? Oh, wait... he's gone awfully quiet, hasn't he?'

Marco's fists clenched. 'You don't know what you're talking about.'

X took a step closer, his smile widening. 'Don't I? I can see it in your eyes. You've already started mourning him. Surly's guilt has been eating away at him, hasn't it? And now he's gone, Marco. Gone because I said so.'

The words hit like a sledgehammer. Marco lunged, his vision narrowing to a tunnel focused solely on X. The fight was brutal and primal. Marco's fists connected with X's face, but X only laughed through the blood. 'This is all you have?' X taunted, landing a vicious blow to Marco's ribs.

The guards remained indifferent, their faces turned away as if they hadn't noticed the violence unfolding before them. Other inmates circled, jeering and shouting, the chaotic din only fuelling Marco's rage.

But X was relentless. Even as Marco pounded into him, he continued his verbal assault. 'Surly was the only part of you worth saving,' he sneered, his voice cutting through the noise.

'And now he's dead. You're nothing but a husk, Marco. A murderer. A fraud.'

Marco's punches faltered. He staggered back, his breath heaving. X's words pierced deeper than any physical blow. He felt a hollowness creeping in, a void where Surly's presence had once been. X, bruised and bloodied, stood tall, triumphant.

'You hear that emptiness, Marco?' X said, his voice now calm, almost soothing. He was a threat, a storm on the brink, ready to unleash at any given moment, and Marco was in the eye of it. 'That's the sound of your undoing. And it's only the beginning.'

And with that, X turned and sauntered away, his footsteps echoing in Marco's ears long after disappearing from sight. The guards moved in, dragging Marco back to his cell, but his mind was elsewhere, replaying every word, every subtle threat.

As cold as a cellar's breath, walls closed around him again, pressing down with a new weight. Only this time, it wasn't the prison making him feel trapped. It was the haunting awareness that someone nearby knew him—knew too much, perhaps—and that this someone was intent on dismantling him piece by piece.

Who was X, really? How did he know so much about Marco? And most unsettling of all, what had Marco done to earn his dark fixation? Marco was no stranger to threats, but this... this felt different. The storm was drawing nearer.

As he settled uneasily into his cell's frigid embrace, Marco couldn't shake the suspicion that, for the first time in years, he was genuinely afraid. Deep down, he knew this was just the first step into something far more sinister—an ordeal that would push him to the edge and force him to confront his own ghosts.

But then, as he stared at the wall, a slow smile crept across his face. Somewhere deep within him, Rip chuckled, his laughter low and menacing.

'Let them come,' Marco murmured. 'We're ready.'

CHAPTER 3
UNRELENTING TORMENT

Time had twisted, slowing and tightening around Marco, suffocating like a noose. Each tick of the clock seemed to be counting down to something inevitable. An oppressive sense of dread gnawed at him in an unfamiliar way, like a shadow he couldn't shake.

Even though Marco hadn't had a physical encounter with X again since that day in the yard, his presence had poisoned the air.

Late at night, when the prison was wrapped in silence, Marco would hear an insidious voice seeping through the cracks of his cell, calling his name in a low and sing-song tone. It threaded through the darkness as if it came from the walls themselves. He tried to convince himself it was a figment of his imagination. But the taunts wove into his dreams until sleep became a prison he couldn't escape.

'Marco... Marco...' the voice would call, echoing in his head even after he jolted awake, beads of sweat forming on his brow. 'You can't hide from me, Marco... I'm right here.'

It continued night after night. Sometimes, it was a whisper; other times, a low chuckle, filling his cell with a suffocating threat. Marco tried to ignore it, covering his head with his thin blanket, but the voice seemed to seep into his bones. His once-familiar surroundings now felt foreign, every shadow a potential threat, every sound amplified in his mind.

One night, unable to bear it any longer, Marco hurled his blanket to the side, leaped from his bunk, and pounded his fists against the icy steel bars.

'Shut up! Shut up, you sick bastard!' he screamed, his voice raw with anger and desperation.

A low, mocking laugh drifted back to him. X's voice, calm and malicious, cut through the silence. 'Oh, Marco... losing your cool?' he taunted. 'With this reaction, you're only making it more fun for me.'

Marco slumped against the door, breathing heavily.

'You thought you could escape, didn't you?' X's voice was conversational, almost amused, each syllable steeped in a quiet but lethal threat. 'Thought maybe you could finally start over, out of sight, out of mind. But I'm here to remind you... there's no escape from your past. You can't run from me, Marco.'

A shiver ran through Marco. He tried to shake it off, telling himself that X was just another inmate, but there was something in those words. Something about how he spoke them... it made Marco's skin crawl. X was different. He wasn't here by coincidence, and the realization gnawed at Marco's mind, feeding his growing paranoia.

He knew this game and had played it himself with his victims, but being on the receiving end was a different kind of torture. His thoughts spun wildly, like a relentless theme park ride he couldn't escape.

Why did they have to put this motherfucker across the hall from me? Jeezus, I can't escape him. He's a few steps away from me. His voice permeates my cell. Worst of all, he's permanently in my head.

'Rip,' Marco muttered, 'where's your ever-contracting advice? Now that I need it, you're quiet. What's up?'

'Rome wasn't built in a day, big man,' Rip replied. 'Hold your horses. I'm working on it.'

No input from Surly. The silence was deafening.

*   *   *

In the days that followed, the torment escalated. It was subtle—a whispered insult here, a knowing smile there—but each encounter chipped away at Marco's resolve. In the yard, he'd feel X's gaze on him, watching, studying, waiting to pounce. Some days, X would stand just close enough to be heard, whispering threats that made Marco's skin prickle.

The guards seemed oblivious, treating X like any other inmate, but Marco knew better. This man was different, more dangerous. He wasn't just another prisoner; he was a predator, and Marco was his target.

Back in the cells, it continued.

'You look nervous, Marco,' X would say, his voice a low murmur as he passed, escorted by guards. 'I can smell your fear. It's intoxicating.'

Later, when it was just the two of them and the shadows, X was relentless.

'You think you're safe in here? Do you think these walls can protect you? They can't. I'm in your head, and I'm not leaving.'

Marco gritted his teeth, ignoring X's voice, but the man grew bolder.

'Did you ever wonder what it's like, Marco? To be hunted? To be the prey? Because that's what you are now. You're mine.'

He tried to block it out, focusing on the book in his hands, but the words on the page blurred, the letters twisting into X's taunts.

* * *

Days turned into weeks, and the torment escalated. X found ways to taunt Marco at every turn. Attempts to ignore him merely seemed to fuel his sadistic enjoyment. Marco began finding cryptic messages in places only he would see: tiny notes slipped beneath his cell door, scraps of paper with phrases like *I'm closer than you think* or *You'll never see it coming.* The messages were short, but they carried an unnerving weight, as though they'd been designed to chip away at his sanity.

Still nothing from Surly. Rip had gone quiet, though Marco could still feel him, lurking in the back of his mind.

One night, as Marco lay in his bunk, the whispers continued—but this time, they were accompanied by a soft scratching sound. Marco tensed, listening closely. The noise was faint but unmistakable, like something being carved into the wall.

Slowly, Marco sat up, his stomach churning. X's voice came to him, low and deliberate.

'Do you hear that, Marco? That's the reality of your end. Every scratch, every mark... counting down the days.'

Marco's eyes darted to the cell opposite his and there, gouged into the concrete wall, were ten scratches, jagged and deep. His pulse quickened as his gaze drifted slowly over each groove, a silent countdown. He spun around abruptly, hoping to erase the image from his mind. But the scratches remained unmistakable.

X's laugh echoed through the cell, chilling Marco to the bone. 'Sweet dreams, Marco. You're going to need them.'

* * *

The next night, Marco found a new scratch slashed through one of the old. The count had reduced to nine.

X was counting down, but to what? What exactly was he planning to do?

Marco slumped against the wall. He could hardly breathe as he stared at the marks, feeling a slow but powerful fear take root in him. He didn't know how X planned to bring about his 'end.' But the question that haunted him, that gnawed at the edges of his sanity, was how X knew so much about him.

As the hours ticked by and the countdown continued, Marco could feel his grip on reality slipping. X had taken things to the next level, and Marco knew, with a sinking feeling, that this would only get worse. The true nightmare had begun, and he was trapped, helpless to stop it. He needed to get out of Steelvale. But he hadn't been able to speak to Eddie in weeks, and he had no way of contacting Noctis on his own. Even Rip's presence was distant.

For the first time in his life, Marco was alone.

Alone... except for X.

Days passed in a surreal haze, and sleep became a battleground. When he closed his eyes, he was haunted by visions of X's face, his cold, mocking smile. When Marco managed to drift off, his dreams were filled with footsteps ringing down endless, dark corridors, X's voice whispering his name, calling him closer and closer to something he couldn't see.

In one of these nightmares, he was running through a labyrinth of shadowed hallways, his panicked breaths echoing in the darkness. And behind him, always just a step away, was X, his laughter filling the air. 'Run, Marco, run!' he called, his voice a blend of mockery and malice. 'But there's no escape... I'm right here.'

Marco would wake up gasping, his heart racing, sweat pouring down his face as the emptiness of his cell pressed in around him. He'd reach out, gripping the freezing metal frame of his bunk, trying to steady himself, but the dread remained a constant companion.

On the seventh night, Marco counted only three marks left intact on the wall. He stared at it, his mouth sour with a desperate mix of fear and anger. X had played and toyed with him, but now his patience was wearing thin. He had survived too much and fought too many battles to let this sadistic monster get the best of him.

That night, Marco decided to confront him. He waited until the lights went out, the prison shrouded in darkness. Then, he moved to the front of his cell, his voice barely a whisper as he called out.

'X... What do you want from me?'

For a moment, silence. Then, soft and insidious, X's voice slipped through the dark.

'What do I want, Marco? I want you to know what it feels like to be targeted. To feel that helpless fear, that despair. And soon... you will.'

'If you're trying to scare me, it's not working.'

X's laugh was a low, mocking sound. 'Oh, I don't need to try, Marco. You're already terrified. I can see it in your eyes and smell it in the air. And when that last mark is slashed... you'll finally understand.'

Marco's blood ran cold. The final scratch was only three days away, and the countdown felt like a ticking bomb, a pulse that thrummed beneath his skin. X wasn't just threatening him. He was promising something, and the question of what he was planning nibbled at Marco's mind, robbing him of what little comfort he had left.

As he lay back on his bunk, the darkness pressing in, he realized he had no choice but to face what was coming.

CHAPTER 4
A FALSE SENSE OF SECURITY

The final hours were slipping away when it happened.

Marco woke to heavy footsteps reverberating down the corridor, stirring unease in his stomach. Steelvale had a brutal predictability; every day blended into the next, marked by the strict routine of guards and meals. It could mean someone was being taken to solitary or, in rare cases, moved to a different facility. But today, something was different—an undercurrent of tension charged the air as the footsteps grew louder and closer.

Pricking his ears, Marco strained to listen. The guards' murmured voices sounded lower than usual, more intense, yet their words slipped out of reach.

But then, he heard it—his tormentor's voice, no longer dripping with malice but tense and unusually resigned.

'Are you serious? *Now?*'

'It's not up for discussion,' a guard replied brusquely. 'Orders from the top.'

The cell door across from Marco's creaked open, and there was silence. Marco's heart pounded in his chest. Was this it? Was the nightmare finally coming to an end?

Marco held his breath. A faint clinking of chains sounded, then a scuffle, and moments later, the guards' footsteps receded, becoming faint echoes in the concrete maze of Steelvale, followed by the distant clanging of a gate. Marco listened for any sign that

X might still be there, but there was nothing. Silence settled over the hall. For the first time in weeks, it felt... peaceful.

He dared to hope.

Hours passed before a guard appeared at Marco's cell. No emotion flickered across his face. He swallowed hard, forcing himself to stay calm as the guard unlocked the door and gestured for him to step out.

'Your mate's gone,' the guard said curtly. 'You're alone now.'

The cell door clicked shut behind him, leaving Marco stunned. Was it true? Was this nightmare finally over?

* * *

The black SUV sliced through the night, tyres humming against the rain-slicked highway. X sat in the back seat, his hands resting loosely on his lap, eyes fixed on the streaks of water racing across the tinted glass. The escort detail up front remained silent, their focus on the road, but the tension in the car was palpable. No one spoke of the risk they were taking, but it loomed over them like a storm cloud.

As they neared the outskirts of Champaign, the city's lights flickered through the darkness, illuminating the path to the police headquarters. X's mind was already deep in the game, calculating his next move. He had spent months inside Steelvale, laying the groundwork, planting the seeds of doubt and fear. Now, it was time for the next phase.

The SUV pulled into the secured parking lot behind Champaign PD. The cool night air hit X when the door clicked open, sharpening his senses. A uniformed officer led him through a side entrance, past rows of desks cluttered with paperwork and half-empty coffee cups. Tired eyes followed him as he moved through the station—some filled with curiosity, others with distrust. X wasn't one of them, and they knew it.

Lieutenant Craig Ryan sat behind his desk, his expression an impenetrable mask. The moment X stepped inside, the door clicked shut behind him.

Craig shifted a stack of files. Across from him, X sat, flipping through Marco Carrera's profile, the pages filled with mugshots, psychological evaluations, and crime scene photos.

Craig exhaled sharply. 'Nine victims. Nine lives erased like they meant nothing. You know exactly what kind of predator we're dealing with. I wouldn't trust him with a breath of air—neither should you.'

X's eyes never left the file. 'I don't trust anyone in Steelvale. And Marco? He's more than a monster—he's a master manipulator. That's why he needs to believe I can outplay him at his own game.'

'And how's that going?' Craig asked, leaning back.

X let out a low, twisted hiss. 'The first phase is complete. The whispers, the tormenting, the psychological erosion—I've cracked Surly. He was the weaker of the two alter egos.'

Craig let out a low whistle. 'And Marco? How's he responding?'

'He's watching, waiting. He doesn't know where the next hit will come from, and that's exactly where I want him. The physical fight in the yard rattled him. But it's not enough.'

Craig's eyes darkened. 'He's up to something. The force knows it. We don't know what, but we can't afford to wait for him to make the first move. We need to find out if he has a confidante inside. Someone he's feeding information to.'

'Then that's my next move. Gain his trust. Let him think I'm the only one who understands him.'

Craig studied him. 'That's a dangerous game. You sure you're ready for it?'

X met his gaze. 'I don't have a choice.'

A beat of silence stretched between them before Craig cleared his throat. 'Your parents—I've kept them in the loop. They're not happy, but they're proud of what you're doing. Grateful.'

Briefly, X looked away, before nodding. 'Good.'

Craig leaned forward. 'Whatever happens, don't forget—you're not alone in this. We've got you covered.'

X inhaled, steadying himself. 'Time for phase two.'

Craig locked eyes with him. 'Stay sharp,' he said firmly. 'Marco's not the only one playing games.'

* * *

The relentless dread that had strangled Marco's sanity finally began to loosen its grip. Though far from perfect, his days settled into something almost peaceful. And yet, beneath it all, the unmoving clock still hovered on the brink. The silence left in X's absence was both a relief and an unsettling void, one Marco couldn't quite ignore. He caught himself glancing toward the empty cell across the hall, half-expecting the man to materialize, ready to pick up where his psychological torment had left off. But the cell remained empty. And slowly—perhaps foolishly—Marco began to lower his guard.

The guards seemed to share in Marco's newfound sense of security. They no longer lingered near his cell and watched him with suspicion. Marco began to move through the prison with a confidence he hadn't felt in weeks.

Until one night.

Marco lay on his bunk, staring at the ceiling, his mind finally quiet. And then he heard it—a faint, almost imperceptible whisper, soft as a breeze.

'Marco...'

He sat bolt upright, his pulse racing, searching the darkness. But the cell was empty. He held his breath and strained his ears, listening intently, but the only sound was the hum of the ventilation.

'Just my imagination,' he muttered, rubbing his eyes, trying to shake off the chill that crept over his skin. But he could not shake the feeling of being watched by something sinister, lurking just out of sight.

* * *

The next night, the whisper returned, louder and more insistent.

'Marco...'

Every muscle in Marco's body tensed. Every breath he took felt like swallowing shards of ice. Every nerve screamed that it couldn't be X. He was gone, moved to another prison—yet the voice was unmistakable. His tormenting whisper was back, taunting Marco in the dead of night, invisible yet somehow inescapable.

By the third night, the familiar fear had settled back over Marco, this time as suffocating as a sealed tomb. He lay in bed, staring at the wall, trying to convince himself that he was safe, that X was gone. Every sound in the prison seemed amplified, every shadow tinged with malice. And then he heard it—something he had hoped he would never hear again.

'Three days, Marco. Three days...'

The blood drained from Marco's face. The countdown hadn't ended;

it had been paused. And now, it had restarted, ticking relentlessly toward something he couldn't see but could intimately feel, nibbling at his sanity. X had managed to burrow into his head from miles away.

Marco scrambled to his feet, pacing his cell. Panic gripped him. His thoughts spiralled, each one darker than the last. X was still pulling the strings from afar, unravelling his fragile sense of security. The countdown etched into the wall felt more real, more menacing, like a spectre looming over his life. Now, every shadow held a threat, every whisper, a promise of doom. Marco's prison had become his tomb, and with each breath, he realized that the man who had haunted him was still very much present in his mind, like an infection spreading through his thoughts.

The next morning, Marco's eyes settled on the countdown on the wall. Three, still. And he knew now, with sickening certainty, that when that count reached zero, he'd be lucky if it was merely his body trapped in Steelvale.

CHAPTER 5
HAUNTING SILENCE

The whispers, once as persistent as a pulse, were now elusive, flickering in and out of Marco's awareness. They haunted his nights, slipping in like fog, seeping into his bones, dissipating just as he reached for them. Each time they vanished, the silence left in their wake felt heavier, darker.

Days bled into weeks, and Steelvale's unforgiving monotony drummed into Marco's spirit. He had constructed a rhythm to survive, a grim routine. Wake. Eat. Watch the window. Eat. Sleep. His was a stark existence, isolated from the other inmates. The oppressive silence engulfed him. Why couldn't Eddie have been placed in the same block? Life would've been infinitely less unbearable. Rip wouldn't speak. Surly was gone. His interactions with the guards were minimal; even to them, he had grown invisible. His damp, dimly lit cell became a place where time seemed to stretch and warp, and his mind was left to wander through endless corridors of its own making.

The small, barred window was his only access to the outside world. Through it, he watched the shifting shadows of daylight dissolve into the murky darkness of the night and roll back in at dawn. Life outside went on with impassive consistency, indifferent to his existence. His sole companions were the occasional shadows flickering past his cell and the distant hum of machinery, which reminded him of life beyond the brutal concrete walls.

Marco Carrera had been forsaken long before Steelvale's iron gates clamped shut behind him. His atrocities had not only stolen lives but severed the one thing that might have tethered him to humanity—his family. There were no letters, no calls, and no whispered inquiries about his wellbeing.

Not a single visitor had crossed Steelvale's threshold to see him. Not one. And nothing would change that.

* * *

One day, something shifted. Marco noticed that the whispers were fading. Their absence was unsettling, leaving a void where he'd once cursed their presence. He tried to shake it off as paranoia, but the air felt heavier, charged, as though something was waiting for him just beyond his reach.

The brittle silence shattered when a guard approached his cell and called him to the warden's office. His gut twisted, and a chill ran through him as he walked down the corridor, flanked by the featureless grey walls of the prison. Each step felt like it brought him closer to the edge of a crisis he wasn't prepared for. When he entered the sterile, fluorescent-lit room, he was greeted by Chase Flannery's piercing gaze. His eyes never left Marco's face as he gestured for him to sit.

Marco Carrera waited stiffly in the cold metal chair, the weight of the moment pressing into him like a vice. Across the desk, Warden Flannery leaned back, rubbing his fingers together with slow, deliberate ease, poker-faced—except for the faintest flicker of satisfaction in his eyes.

'Carrera,' Flannery said. 'After a recent review, your execution date has been moved up. It's time you prepared for what's coming.'

The words sliced through the air, sharp as a blade. Marco barely masked the jolt that ran through him. His mind struggled to process the implications, but the reality was inescapable.

Flannery's lips curled into something that wasn't quite a smile. 'Speechless? That's a first.'

Marco inhaled slowly, gripping the arms of the chair, anchoring himself to something real. He had been so consumed by the whispers that his execution date had faded into the deepest recesses of his mind. His thoughts swirled, and he struggled to grasp the implications, but the reality remained, carved in stone by Flannery's hard gaze. He wouldn't give Flannery the satisfaction of seeing him unravel.

The warden leaned forward. 'You didn't actually think you'd slither your way out of this, did you?' He scoffed. 'Nine bodies, Carrera. Nine lives wiped out because of you. Your little games, your smug superiority—it ends soon.'

Anger twitched beneath Marco's cheekbones, but he stayed silent.

Flannery tilted his head. 'No snarky words? No clever quips? That's disappointing. I figured you'd at least try to manipulate your way out of this one.' He let out a low chuckle. 'Guess even you know there's no way out.'

Marco forced his expression into a mask of indifference. Flannery leaned in further, dropping his voice to a near whisper. 'You want to know the best part? No one gives a shit. Not a single soul is fighting for you. Your mother's gone—died knowing what a monster she raised. Your father? He washed his hands of you the second the cuffs clicked around your wrists. No visitors. No appeals. No last-minute rescues. You die alone, Carrera.'

Marco swallowed, forcing down the sting in his throat.

A slow, satisfied exhale left Flannery's lips as he sat back. 'I'll be there, front row. Watching as you take your last breath. And I'll enjoy every second of it.'

Marco held the warden's gaze. He didn't flinch or blink—just let the silence stretch - taut, loaded with unspoken contempt.

Shades of Craig. The words slithered through his mind, bitter and mocking. *Always the same recycled lines, like they're reading from a goddamn script. 'I'll be there. Prepare for the end. It's time.' Blah, blah, blah.* He almost sneered, amusement thin and cruel. *Do they ever come up with something original, or is this just the standard farewell speech before the needle drops? Pathetic!*

The warden tapped his fingers against the desk. 'Do you have any questions?'

A slow smile crept onto Marco's face, a final act of defiance. 'Yeah,' he said, voice calm despite the storm raging inside. 'What will you do with yourself when I'm gone?'

Flannery didn't falter. 'Oh, I'll sleep just fine.'

Marco held the warden's gaze for a long, tense moment. Then, finally, he nodded. He had nothing left to say.

'Take him back,' Flannery ordered. There was a cruel pleasure woven through his tone.

As the guards yanked Marco to his feet, claustrophobia settled over him. The walls of Steelvale seemed smaller now, closing in. No matter how many games he had played or how many moves he had calculated, there was no escape this time. He fell onto his bunk, staring at the ceiling. The whispers, which had once plagued him like demons, now seemed insignificant—a mockery of his true fate. Every threat, every taunt, all of it felt small in comparison to the looming spectre of his own death.

With each passing hour, the silence grew more unbearable,

amplifying every racing thought, every muted fear, until Marco was trapped in a suffocating loop of dread.

* * *

The days dragged by. Marco glanced at the empty space opposite him, half expecting to see the familiar dark eyes and twisted smile of the tormentor he'd come to despise. But the cell remained empty, as silent as a tomb. The relentless march toward his execution was no longer a looming danger but an imminent reality, and in that silence, Marco faced the terrifying weight of his mortality.

He wondered if X's departure was just another cruel twist in a game that was far from over.

In the stillness of his cell, Marco found himself haunted not by the whispers but by the overwhelming quiet. Surly had deserted him, and where was Rip when Marco needed him? They had once shared his warped world, which had been a twisted kind of comfort in the echoing loneliness—and that comfort had vanished. He was adrift in a sea of helplessness and isolation.

CHAPTER 6
ECHOES OF AGONY

Four weeks of uneasy peace had dulled the whispers.

Until tonight.

Steelvale had always prided itself on its iron grip—strict routines, private cells, and an unyielding structure designed to break men before they ever had a chance to break free. But even a fortress had its cracks.

The prison had long been due for a renovation. Not just for fresh paint and new concrete, but to reinforce its order. Entire cell blocks were gutted, ventilation systems torn apart, and security infrastructure reworked. Yet, as weeks dragged by, what started as a project to modernize Steelvale had become a logistical nightmare. Delays mounted. Costs spiralled.

And the prison population kept growing.

With numbers reaching critical levels, Steelvale's administration had to abandon the one-inmate-per-cell rule. Double-bunking became inevitable.

Marco had overheard the murmurs—guards grumbling in passing, inmates speculating in the yard. No one wanted a cellmate. For some, it was an inconvenience. For others, it was a death sentence.

He never thought he'd be one of the unlucky ones.

Yet here he stood, watching the guards drag in a rusted metal bunk, its screeching legs carving into the floor like nails on bone.

The air inside his cell shifted. The last light faded from the narrow window. A familiar chill slithered down his spine. His heart slammed against his ribs.

Then he heard it. A voice he knew too well.

X was back.

Not a ghost. Not a memory. Flesh and blood.

And Marco was trapped.

X's shadow stretched across the stained concrete floor as he stepped into Marco's cell, flanked by two guards. Marco felt his skin crawl as X's malevolent gaze fixed on him, lips twisted into a smile that dripped with contempt and sadistic delight. Marco's instinct was to retreat, but the walls pressed close, and he had nowhere to hide.

'So, we meet again, Carrera,' X drawled, his voice a venomous purr. The door clanged shut behind him, sealing Marco's fate.

The silence that followed was suffocating, punctuated only by X's heavy, deliberate steps closing the distance between them. Hatred radiated from him, raw and unfiltered.

'Did you think you'd get away with it?' X sneered. 'All those years. All those lives. The whispers told me you'd pay, and now you're going to.'

Before Marco could process the threat, X lunged, his hand a blur as he grabbed Marco by the collar and slammed him against the wall. Marco's vision blackened, the impact reverberating through his body as X's fist connected with his jaw. He gasped for breath, but X didn't relent. Blow after blow rained down with vicious precision, each more brutal than the last. Blood smeared across the cold floor as X released Marco and he collapsed.

X had a dark presence that seemed to swallow the room whole, his eyes bright with a malevolent glimmer. Marco's heartbeat surged.

Without warning, X lunged at him again. He scrambled to defend himself, but the attacks came in a swift flurry of rage. The pain was sharp and unrelenting, a brutal reminder of the power imbalance that Marco had once held over his victims.

'Do you remember Ava?' X hissed. 'Young, beautiful Ava. A wonderful soul inside and out, and sadly so madly in love with you. The girl who trusted you. Who thought you were some kind of hero. You tore her apart, Carrera. She never even stood a chance. You made sure of that, deciding her life didn't matter. '

Marco squeezed his stinging eyes shut, but X's voice was relentless, clawing at his sanity.

'And how about Mia? The one whose body you kept, like some twisted souvenir. Not to mention Harper. Why did she bear the brunt of your rage? That intrigued me, I have to say. Did you even care about her when you—'

X cut himself off, as if strangled for a moment by his own rage, and dragged in a sharp breath.

'Then there was little Summer,' he continued; every syllable dripped with scorn. 'Just a child, sweet and innocent, and yet you ended her life with such cold precision. Do you honestly believe she still thought it was a game until the end? And Holly... she almost got you, didn't she? Too much of a challenge for your weak, sadistic ego.'

X laughed, low and cold, the sound of pure malice. 'And Grace Rose. Poor, young Grace, just a schoolgirl. You're deranged, Carrera. To even prey on schoolgirls. Fuck, you really *are* sick. You left nothing but corpses and shattered lives in your wake, and you think you deserve peace? You're delusional.'

Marco clutched his head, trying to drown out X's words, but it was futile. Each name sliced at his mind like razors, dredging up memories he thought he had buried. He remembered their faces, their last moments—moments he had ended. His resolve was crumbling, the walls he had built around his memories collapsing under the force of X's accusations.

X leaned over Marco, his voice a poisonous snarl. 'Oh, we're only getting warmed up. Those were just the girls from the start of your killing spree, Carrera. Your little practice run, right? Now, let's focus on the ones that supposedly mattered—the ones with everything to lose, the high-profile cases.'

He delivered a vicious kick to Marco's ribs, before continuing, his tone now conversational.

'I've never been able to fully wrap my head around all this. So, why did you decide to step up a notch—or three? What drove you to go after the big guns? Were you starstruck, or operating on a different level than I first thought? I'll give you credit where it's due; you showed some serious nerve there. Bravo!'

X's mocking claps echoed through the cell.

'A few more questions while we're on the subject. Why Leigh? Are you anti-sports or something? Or was she not good enough in bed? Care to elaborate—nudge, nudge, wink, wink?' With each word, he drove his shoe into Marco's aching stomach. 'I must admit, Gabriella was hot. What made you want to kill her? Did things not work out with her? Or were you too blinded by your ego to worry that her fame might expose you? And what about her close-knit family? Jeezus, you've got a pair and a half, I'll give you that!' Now X's kicks targeted Marco's crotch, nearly blinding him with pain.

'And then there's Anastasia, the cool one with all that spunk. Why take her out? She could've written a song about you. That's where you fucked up, buddy. A trifecta? A bold move for a betting man. They all could have made something of themselves, but you snuffed out their lights, didn't you?' X crouched down and leaned in close, his voice a hiss in Marco's ear. 'But you didn't care, and you failed to hide the mess. You were addicted to the power, to the thrill. Thought you were untouchable, but look at you now.' His smile twisted cruelly. 'They're all gone because of you. But in here? You're nothing. Just a rat waiting to be crushed.'

Bile rose in Marco's throat at the twisted symphony of his crimes, the grotesque reminder of the lives he'd destroyed. Memories of his victims danced before his eyes, their faces haunting him, accusing him. He felt his sins like a physical force, each a knife twisting in his chest. And when X's foot began laying into him again, his pleas for mercy were met with mocking laughter. He tried to call for the guards, but the oppressive silence of the corridor swallowed his voice. X's blows were deliberate and timed to perfection, leaving Marco helpless.

As the minutes dragged on, Marco's desperation intensified. The physical violence had pushed him to the brink of insanity, and he found himself begging his tormentor, his voice quivering with fear, a raw whisper escaping his lips. 'Please... stop. I'll do anything. Just stop!'

And then, as suddenly as it had begun, the assault ended. X moved away, and Marco slumped to the floor, his body bruised and broken, his mind a fractured mess of guilt and terror. He looked up through swollen eyes, catching sight of X's smirk, the triumph in his gaze.

'Pathetic,' X muttered, turning his back on Marco. 'All those lives, and here you are, begging for mercy. You're not even worth the air you breathe.'

In the following hours, Marco's mind raced with the idea of confronting the warden. His fragile sense of stability had been shattered, and he could no longer wait passively. X's sudden return had assured him that he couldn't endure this suffering; he needed to find a way out, and he needed his former strength to raise its ugly head and see him through his remaining days. The only path he saw was through the warden's intervention.

* * *

The moment Marco stepped into their cell after his time in the yard the next day, X struck. He launched at Marco with brutal precision, slamming him against the unforgiving concrete wall.

When it was finally over, and X had left for his own time outside, Marco forced himself upright. His ribs screamed in protest, every breath a jagged blade slicing through his side. He had reached his limit; he'd been beaten one too many times with no consequences.

I'm not letting this slide any longer. Action needs to be taken. Immediately.

Slamming his fist against the call button inside his cell, he waited. When the guard finally arrived, Marco locked eyes with him. 'I need to see Warden Flannery. Now.'

The guard arched a sceptical brow. 'What for?'

'That's between me and him.'

There must have been something in Marco's voice—a finality, a broken edge—that convinced the guard not to argue. Ten minutes later, Marco found himself sitting before Warden Flannery's massive oak desk, the stale scent of cigars clinging to the air. The warden barely spared him a glance as he flipped through paperwork.

'This better be good, inmate,' Flannery said. 'I've got a schedule to keep.'

Marco leaned forward, gripping the edge of the desk. 'I want you to bring my execution date forward.'

Flannery's hand stilled over a page. Slowly, he looked up, eyes narrowing. 'Excuse me?'

'You heard me,' Marco said, his voice devoid of fear. 'I'm done. I can't take this anymore. Move it up. Make the call.'

A smirk tugged at the corner of Flannery's mouth. He leaned back in his chair, lacing his fingers together. 'You think that's how this works?'

'I know you have connections. There's got to be a way—'

'Carrera,' Flannery interrupted, shaking his head, 'even if I gave a damn, which I don't, the state doesn't move on a whim. Reviews, appeals, logistics—these things take months, sometimes years. You wanting to tap out early doesn't change that.'

Marco dug his nails into the wood. 'I'm not asking for a favour. I'm telling you I can't do this anymore.'

Flannery sighed, rubbing his temples as if Marco's mere presence exhausted him. 'And why should I care? Because your cellmate is handing you your ass every night? You think you're the first man in here to get roughed up?'

'This isn't living. This is slow torture.'

'And?'

Marco swallowed hard. 'And I'm asking you—begging you—to put an end to it.'

For a moment, silence stretched between them, thick and suffocating. Then, Flannery barked out a humourless laugh. 'Jesus, you really think you're special, don't you? Listen, inmate. You don't get to call the shots. You take what's given, and you endure.' He leaned forward, his voice lowering. 'Grow a pair, Carrera. Take each day as it comes. And don't waste my damn time again.'

Flannery pressed a button on his intercom. 'Take him back to his cell.'

The guards reappeared, gripping Marco's arms and hauling him to his feet. He didn't fight them. What was the point?

Flannery's voice followed Marco as they dragged him away. 'Next time you want to complain, save us both the trouble and keep it to yourself.'

The door slammed shut behind him.

* * *

In the following days, Marco began to craft a plan, one that was both desperate and dangerous. He would use the very chaos his tormentor had unleashed to his advantage. If he couldn't find peace through his execution, he would find a way to turn X's tactics against him. The warden and the prison staff would be his new targets, and Marco was prepared to play the final hand in this deadly game of revenge.

CHAPTER 7
SCHEMES IN THE SHADOWS

The prison yard was alive with murmurs, imminent fights, and men who had lost their humanity long before the bars had caged them. Marco and Eddie were different. They had purpose.

Marco locked onto Eddie at the far end of the yard and strode toward him, as casually as his injuries would allow, his pulse steady.

'Another beautiful day in paradise, and you sure do blend in well,' Marco muttered, stopping beside him.

Sarcasm danced on Eddie's lips. 'Would you prefer I wear a neon sign?'

'The storm's rolling in.'

'The kind you dance in or the kind that drowns you?'

Marco's gaze darted to the guard tower, then to Eddie. His voice was low, urgent. 'My new cellie pummels me every night. I don't know how much more of this shit I can take.' He exhaled sharply, jaw tight. 'I've started playing along, letting him think he's won—buying time. But we need to move. Fast. We gotta get the hell outta here before it's too late.' Marco shifted his weight slightly, his voice just loud enough to be heard over the hum of the other inmates. 'Any news from the Cabal since we last spoke?'

'Apparently, it's hectic with other shit going down. Word is we gotta hang on. When the wind shifts north, we'll move.'

'North, huh? Bit of a gamble, don't you think?'

'Not if we time it right.' Eddie flicked his eyes toward the guard tower. 'We slip through when the hounds take their nap.'

Marco nodded, adjusting his stance like he was just stretching his legs. 'I assume our mutual friend still has the keys to the front gate?'

'Friend's a strong word. But he's motivated.'

Marco's lips twitched. 'Motivated, or just scared of you?'

Eddie didn't answer. Instead, he glanced at a group of prisoners laughing too close to the fence. One wrong word, one wrong look, and their whole plan could go up in smoke. He cracked his knuckles, a subtle signal. 'You sure this is the right call?'

Marco exhaled slowly. 'Door's open. We walk through or we rot.' He followed Eddie's gaze. 'You worried?'

Eddie shook his head. 'You?'

Marco chuckled. 'Hell no. With you by my side, I know it's only a matter of time.'

The guard at the far end turned his back, just when Marco expected.

'See that? There's our cue when it's go time. Shit, man, wish we didn't have to wait so long.'

'Patience.' Eddie's voice was a whisper now, but Marco caught it. Eddie cracked his knuckles again, the sound sharp and deliberate. Then, louder, for anyone listening: 'Think I'll try for extra pudding at lunch. Feels like a good day for it.'

A chuckle curled at the edge of his grin. 'You always were an optimist.'

They parted just as the yard alarm blared, signalling the end of their brief freedom.

* * *

X sat in the rigid metal chair, his fingers drumming lightly against the scratched surface of the visitation table. The reinforced glass in front of him reflected a weary face—his own—but his eyes sharpened when the heavy door on the other side creaked open.

His mother entered first. She was smaller than he remembered, bundled in a heavy cardigan, her silver-streaked hair pinned back in a neat bun. His father followed, shoulders squared, his walk purposeful, but his lined face betrayed the weight he carried.

The second his mother's eyes found X's, they filled with tears. She rushed forward, placing both hands against the glass as if she could reach through and pull him into her arms.

'Oh, my boy,' she whispered. 'Look at you... What have they done to you?'

X forced a small smile. 'I'm fine, Ma. Really.'

His father bit down on whatever he was about to say as he sat beside her, his hands folded tightly on the table. 'This isn't right,' he muttered. 'You don't belong here.'

X leaned forward, lowering his voice. 'I'm exactly where I need to be.'

His mother shook her head, blinking away tears. 'But why, son? Why would you do this? Why put yourself in harm's way?'

X exhaled, choosing his words carefully. 'Because someone has to. You know what happened—the lives stolen, the futures erased. The real monsters in here? They don't fear the law. They don't fear justice. They only fear what lurks inside these walls with them. That's where I come in.'

His father's expression hardened. 'And what about the families left behind? The ones still grieving? Throwing yourself into this hellhole—have you thought about what that really means?' His voice cracked on the last word, but he quickly masked it.

'That's why I needed to see you,' X said, swallowing the lump in his throat. 'To make sure you're both okay. To know I still have a home to come back to when this is over.'

His mother shook her head, voice trembling. 'But at what cost, my darling? How much of yourself will be left when you walk out of here?'

X hesitated. The truth was, he didn't know. But doubt was a luxury he couldn't afford.

'I need you to trust me,' he said, voice steady. 'I'm entrenched in this—there's no way out now. I'm making progress. I have a mission to fulfill, and I won't stop until it's done.'

His father's knuckles whitened as he gripped the edge of the table. 'And if they find out who you really are?'

X gave a tight smile. 'Then I make sure they don't live to tell the tale.'

His mother gasped, pressing a hand to her chest. 'Don't talk like that.'

'Ma,' he said gently, 'I need you both to call me twice a week. Stay in the loop. Let me know you're safe.'

His father exhaled sharply, then nodded. 'Twice a week.'

X looked at his mother. 'Promise me.'

Her lip quivered, but she said, 'I promise.'

The steel door buzzed behind them. Time was up.

His mother pressed her fingers to her lips, then touched them to the glass. 'Come back to us,' she whispered.

X's throat tightened, but he forced another smile. 'I always do.'

And then they were gone, the chill of cement pressing in the room, leaving X alone with nothing but the reflection of a man he hoped to still recognize when this was all over.

But for now, he had unfinished business.

CHAPTER 8
EVIL'S ALGORITHM

Warden Flannery sat rigidly in the back of the unmarked car, watching the cityscape of Champaign blur past. The trip from Steelvale had been long but necessary. Something wasn't right—he felt it deep in his bones. Craig had insisted on this meeting, and Flannery wasn't one to ignore a man who knew Marco's mind almost as well as the killer did himself.

Flannery stepped into Champaign PD and was immediately greeted by the scent of stale coffee and worn leather. He had left the high-security walls of Steelvale behind for one reason: to uncover what had been eluding him in Marco's case. The files, the reports, the psychological evaluations—he had scoured them all, over and over, yet something was missing. He could feel it like a splinter in his mind, just out of reach.

Minutes later, Flannery leaned back in his chair as he surveyed the two people across from him—Lieutenant Craig Ryan and Kirsten Wells, the former Chicago PD detective turned investigative journalist. If anyone could help him uncover what he had missed, it was them.

The murky glow of old fluorescents cast long shadows across the table. Flannery rubbed his temples, exhaustion evident in his eyes. 'I've gone through Marco's files a million times. Something's missing. I know it. I can feel it.'

Kirsten folded her arms, her piercing gaze fixed on Flannery.

'And you're only just realizing this now? Craig and I have been saying this for years. This isn't just about Marco. It's about who he's connected to.'

'A cabal,' Craig muttered, his voice laced with unease. Flannery raised an eyebrow. 'You look like you don't believe it, but I've seen too much to dismiss the idea. Marco has ties to people who can pull strings even from behind bars.'

Kirsten leaned in. 'He's always been ten steps ahead, Flannery. The letters, the riddles—he taunted us during the investigation. We believe that to him, Steelvale isn't a cage, just a temporary inconvenience.'

Flannery sighed. 'Then let's talk connections. Craig, you were close to the victims' families. What did you pick up? Anything that ties back to Marco's bigger game?'

Craig's face darkened. 'Leigh O'Rielly. Gabriella Cantrello. Anastasia Carlyle-Benson. Three families torn apart. And Marco made sure I felt every second of their grief. You think he sent those letters just to mess with my head? No. They were breadcrumbs. Clues wrapped in torment.'

Kirsten nodded. 'He knew how much they meant to you. That's why he targeted you. And Alessandro. Marco didn't just kill Gabriella—he sent a message to her brother. Pushed him straight into law enforcement.'

Flannery's brows furrowed. 'So, Alessandro becoming a detective wasn't a coincidence?'

'Not even close,' Craig said. 'Marco made sure he had our attention. And now, he wants us to know he's still in control.'

'You'll want to see this.' Kirsten pulled out a folder, sliding it across the table. 'Recent chatter from our sources in Europe— Alessandro's been digging deep. Marco still has allies outside. His reach extends far beyond Steelvale. And this cabal? This... Noctis? They might be his insurance policy.'

Flannery flipped through the pages. 'Damn it. I knew he had influence, but this? If we don't cut him off at the root, it won't matter how many walls Steelvale has.'

'Look at the financial transactions in that file,' Craig said. 'Marco had millions funnelled into offshore accounts before his arrest—money that didn't just vanish. And guess who's been moving those funds since he's been locked up? Individuals tied to suspected Noctis operatives.'

Kirsten tapped a name in the document. 'Vincenzo de Luca. We believe he's one of Noctis's biggest players in Europe. He was in the same circles as Marco before the three high-profile murders. They weren't just business associates; they were part of something bigger. We deciphered encrypted messages between Marco and one of de Luca's top enforcers that were sent just weeks before his arrest. Whatever they were working on, it didn't stop when Marco went to prison.'

Flannery's expression tightened. 'So, you're saying Noctis didn't just support him before—he's still working with them from the inside?'

Craig nodded. 'That's exactly what we're saying. We've had recent reports of key witnesses going missing—people who could have testified about Marco's financial dealings. They disappear, bodies never found. That's not a coincidence. That's a cleanup.'

'And let's not forget the guards,' Kirsten said, her eyes narrowing. 'The ones who suddenly got generous payouts before resigning. Steelvale is maximum security, but Marco doesn't need a key if he owns the people holding the locks.'

'Damn it.' Flannery clenched his fists. 'This isn't just about keeping him contained. If Marco has Noctis behind him, Steelvale isn't a prison—it's his headquarters.'

'Then let's stop talking and start doing,' Craig said grimly. 'If Marco's playing a long game, we need to be ahead of him. We go after Noctis. We find his connections. We burn it all down.'

A flicker of amusement tugged at Kirsten's lips. 'Now that's the Craig I know.'

Flannery exhaled. 'Alright. I'll take this back to Steelvale, but I want everything you've got on Noctis. It's time to dismantle Marco's empire, brick by brick.'

Craig's eyes burned with determination. 'And we'll bury the bastard once and for all.'

CHAPTER 9
THE ART OF DECEPTION

Flannery returned to Steelvale, his head spinning from the revelations of his meeting with Craig and Kirsten. The weight of what he had learned settled deep in his gut. Marco wasn't just a dangerous inmate—he was a puppet master, pulling strings beyond the prison walls. Noctis's reach was longer than he had imagined, which meant tactics had to change. Immediately. So much for him being this weak loner. That was nothing but a façade—one they had all bought into for too long.

Flannery stormed into his office and picked up the phone. 'Get X in here. Now.'

Minutes later, X stepped in. Emotion didn't touch his face—only silence, as always. He sat down without being asked, legs stretched out, exuding the calm of a man who had seen and done things most wouldn't dare to imagine.

Flannery leaned forward, his voice low and firm. 'New plan. The beatings stop. Effective immediately.'

X raised an eyebrow. 'That so?'

'Yes,' Flannery said, holding X's gaze. 'We've been going at this the wrong way. Marco's too smart for brute force. He's got connections—dangerous ones. We need a different approach.'

'And let me guess, you want me to play nice?'

'Not just nice,' Flannery said, steepling his fingers. 'You need to become his friend.'

X let out a low whistle. 'That's a hell of a shift, Warden.'

'It has to be done. Marco's manipulative, but he's also arrogant. If he thinks he's won you over, he may slip and possibly even talk.'

X chuckled. 'So, I let him think I'm coming around to his way of thinking?'

'Exactly,' Flannery said. 'You need to convince him that you see remorse in him. That you believe he's misunderstood. He needs to trust you.'

'I'll give it a shot,' X said, scratching his chin. 'But you do realize if he sees through this, he'll flip the game on me.'

'Then don't let him. And while you're at it, I need you to sniff around the guards. There's a good chance we've got a few dirty ones on payroll.'

X's grin widened. 'Oh, now that part sounds fun.'

'Don't get cocky,' Flannery warned. 'We don't know who's compromised yet, and I don't want you ending up in a body bag.'

X stood, stretching. 'Noted, boss. Anything else?'

'Kirsten is investigating Noctis. Craig's flying to Italy to meet with Alessandro. They're pulling at the threads. We need to make sure nothing unravels on our end.'

'Got it. Now, if you'll excuse me, I've got a psychopath to befriend.'

* * *

The mess hall buzzed with Steelvale's usual chaotic energy. Trays clattered, conversations hummed, and the occasional shove or glare threatened to spark violence. X moved through the crowd with practiced ease, his eyes scanning for anything out of place.

He slid into a seat across from Lenny 'Two-Tooth' Vargas, a veteran inmate with an uncanny ability to sniff out secrets. 'What's the word, Lenny?'

Lenny speared a lump of what barely passed as meatloaf. 'Depends. You looking for business or pleasure?'

'Bit of both,' X said, keeping his tone casual. 'Heard there's been some extra cash floating around. Any idea whose pockets are getting lined?'

Lenny chuckled, his two remaining teeth flashing. 'Oh, you know how it is. Some folks get lucky at poker. Others... get lucky in ways they shouldn't.'

X leaned in. 'I'm not in the mood for riddles, Lenny.'

Lenny wiped his mouth, glancing around before lowering his voice. 'Word is, a couple of guards been real friendly with certain inmates. Packages going in and out, people getting moved to different blocks when it don't make sense.'

'Names?'

Lenny shrugged. 'Come on, man. You know how this works. Information costs.'

'And you know how *I* work,' X said, letting out a mirthless laugh. Tell me now, or I'll make sure your next meal comes with a side of broken fingers.'

Lenny sighed dramatically. 'Alright, alright. Jackson and Meyers. They've been taking late-night walks near C Block. Something's up.'

Standing, X nodded. 'Good man, Lenny. Try not to choke on that mystery meat.'

Lenny grinned. 'No promises.'

As X made his way back across the yard, he felt the shift in the air. Marco had power here—more than anyone had realized. But power could be manipulated. And X would make sure Marco's world crumbled from the inside out.

CHAPTER 10
SHIFTING LOYALTIES

The cell was bathed in a dim, flickering glow, stale with the mingled scents of damp concrete and unwashed bodies. X sat on his bunk, watching Marco with the ease of a man who had spent years analysing people. Marco was sitting on his own bunk, idly flipping through a worn paperback. Whatever he felt was buried deep.

It had been days since the last beating, and X had played his part perfectly. The aggression had vanished, replaced with curiosity, conversation, and a quiet understanding. X knew the best way to break someone wasn't through fists—it was through trust.

'You ever think about what you'll do if you get out of here?' X asked, his tone casual.

Marco didn't look up. 'Not much point thinking about something that's never gonna happen.'

'I don't know,' X said, leaning back against the wall. 'You're a smart guy. Smarter than most in this dump. If anyone could figure a way out—legal or otherwise—it's you.'

Finally, Marco met his gaze. 'Why the sudden interest?'

X shrugged, his expression thoughtful. 'I've been turning things over in my head these past few days. About you. About everything I thought I knew.'

Marco raised an eyebrow.

X continued, voice measured. 'I've spent years sizing people up, figuring out what makes them tick. And I was sure I had you pegged—a manipulator, a guy who only looks out for himself. But maybe I got it wrong. Maybe there's more to you than I thought.'

Though Marco's grin didn't reach his eyes, it didn't need to. There was scepticism in his eyes. 'That so?'

'Yeah. I've seen real monsters here—men who don't think twice about what they've done, who sleep just fine at night. But you? You carry something different. Regret, maybe. Or maybe the weight of decisions that weren't really yours to make... I don't know. You don't talk like a guy who's proud of what he's done.'

Marco exhaled through his nose, tossing his book aside. 'You a shrink now, X? Getting sentimental on me?'

X chuckled. 'Nah. Just saying, maybe you're not the man I thought you were.'

Marco studied him, his gaze sharp, calculating. X could see the gears turning. Was this real? Or was it just another move in the game? A shift was happening—subtle, but palpable. The question was, who was shifting whom?

After a long silence, Marco stood up. 'Come on. Let's hit the yard.'

The yard was a swirling mass of bodies, crackling with tension. Marco led the way, his steps measured, his eyes constantly scanning. X walked beside him, relaxed but alert. Across the yard, Eddie stood by the fence, his usual place of observation, arms folded. Marco's gaze locked onto Eddie. He stared, blank and impenetrable.

'You wanted to meet him,' Marco said. 'Here's your chance. But five minutes, then you're gone.'

'Fair enough.'

As they approached, Eddie's sharp eyes flicked between the two of them. His stance remained rigid, his expression guarded.

'The hell is this?' Eddie muttered.

Marco sighed. 'Relax. He's cool.'

'Cool?' Eddie scoffed. 'The same guy who used you as a punching bag a week ago?' He narrowed his eyes at X. 'I don't buy it.'

Marco crossed his arms. 'Things change.'

'Nah,' Eddie said. 'Not that fast. And you need to be careful, Marco. Don't get sucked into whatever game this is.'

Marco exhaled, glancing sideways at X. 'He's been solid the last few days. We've talked. He's... different.'

Eddie ground his teeth. 'And why have the beatings stopped?'

'Because,' X said slowly, 'we've seen another side of each other, and it makes for easier coexistence.'

Eddie leaned in. 'Just don't say anything you'll regret.'

X checked his watch. 'Time's up. See ya around.' He turned and strode off, leaving Marco and Eddie alone.

Eddie glanced around, then lowered his voice. 'Noctis made contact. We've got two more guards on board.'

'That means we can move sooner. What else?'

'The transport schedules have been altered in our favour. There's a new opening in the security detail on Thursday—three-minute window.'

'Then we need to be damn careful.'

Eddie's face darkened. 'And we can't let X anywhere near this.'

Marco hesitated before nodding. 'Agreed. We move soon. No mistakes.'

Every day in Steelvale had been a test of endurance. But Marco wasn't just enduring—he was planning. In the deepest recesses of his mind, he had been assembling a weapon more dangerous than any shiv or smuggled blade. His escape wouldn't be about brute force. It would be about deception. About precision. And

when the moment came, it wouldn't just be an escape.
It would be an execution.

CHAPTER 11
A DANGEROUS ALLIANCE

*C*raig adjusted his seatbelt as the plane began its descent into Sanremo. The twinkling lights of the Italian Riviera spread below him like a sea of fallen stars. He had no time for the picturesque views, though. His mind was locked onto one thing—Marco.

The moment the wheels touched the tarmac, Craig switched his phone back on. A message from Alessandro awaited him.

I'm waiting for you at Dolce Divino. Corso Imperatrice 10. See ya soon.

Within thirty minutes, Craig was stepping into a dimly lit trattoria tucked away from the main streets. The rich aroma of fresh basil and wood-fired pizza wafted through the restaurant, wrapping everything in its warmth. Alessandro, nursing an espresso, looked up and signalled to Craig. He looked different—stronger, leaner. His sharp suit did little to hide the defined muscle beneath.

'You've been busy,' Craig remarked, sliding into the seat across from him.

A sliver of a smile, sharp as a blade, flickered across Alessandro's face. 'Giovanni doesn't take it easy on anyone. If I wanted to get stronger, I had to earn it.'

'Clearly, you did.' Craig leaned in. 'What do you have for me?'

'More than I expected,' Alessandro said quietly. 'I've been

digging deep, calling in every favour. My reach extends further now—local law enforcement, Interpol... and beyond.'

'Beyond?'

Alessandro hesitated for a moment, then exhaled. 'I have contacts in the CIA.'

Craig's expression remained unreadable, but inside his head, gears were turning. Alessandro had levelled up, and that meant more access—more intel. 'And what have you learned?'

'Marco is playing a dangerous game, but he's not alone. You were right—something is brewing. And I think it starts with Steelvale.'

'I have the same feeling,' Craig said grimly. 'X has been feeding me updates, and the cards are stacked. Noctis is involved.'

Alessandro's face grew shadowed. 'Then Marco isn't just playing with criminals. He's in bed with a global power structure. That changes everything.'

'Which brings me to Eddie.' Craig leaned back. 'Edward Johnson. One of Marco's mates in Steelvale. I've gone through every system with a fine-tooth comb. The guy doesn't exist. No prints, no documentation. Nothing, nada, zilch.'

Alessandro pulled out his phone and dialled a number. A low, clipped conversation followed in Italian. Then, he hung up, his expression grave.

'Eddie's real name is Paulo Carducci.'

Craig narrowed his eyes. 'Never heard of him.'

'That's because he's a ghost. A former Mafia hitman out of Queens. A killer with a rap sheet as long as the Nile. He disappeared ten years ago when he got involved with Noctis.'

'Marco isn't playing with small fry,' Craig muttered, his stomach knotting. 'He has access to serious power and resources. But the question is—who else is involved?'

Alessandro drummed his fingers on the table. 'We need to get ahead of this. Fast.'

* * *

Music pulsed through the underground club, a dark, smoky enclave known in the underworld as the beating heart of Noctis's local operations in Champaign.

Kirsten adjusted her platinum-blonde wig, ensuring it stayed secure beneath the dim, flickering lights. Her disguise was impeccable—green contact lenses, a plunging black dress, and heels that gave her an air of effortless confidence. Her partner for the night, one of Craig's undercover operatives, leaned in and murmured, 'Remember, we're just another rich couple looking for a good time. Blend in.'

She nodded and sipped her cocktail, scanning the room. Dangerous men lounged in velvet booths, their hushed conversations drowned by the bass-heavy music. The scent of expensive cigars and whiskey lingered in the air.

After a waitress sauntered past with a tray of drinks, Kirsten took the opportunity to slip away toward a private corridor marked 'Staff Only.' Her heartbeat thrummed as she pushed through the door, stepping into the unknown.

A long hallway stretched ahead, dimly lit and lined with unmarked doors. Voices filtered from behind one of them—low, tense, unmistakably discussing Marco. She edged closer, pressing herself against the wall.

'We move on Steelvale soon. Ned is handling logistics. Marco and Paulo will have everything they need.'

Paulo?

Kirsten's pulse spiked. Could Eddie and Paulo be one and the same? Or was there more to the mystery?

A sound behind her made her whirl around. A towering bouncer had appeared, eyes narrowing in suspicion.

'Lost, sweetheart?'

Kirsten forced a breathless smile, slipping into her role effortlessly. 'Sorry, babe.' She swayed slightly, feigning drunkenness. 'Looking for the ladies' room.'

The bouncer grunted, unimpressed. 'That way. And don't wander again.'

She stumbled away, her heart hammering. She needed to get this intel back to Craig—and pronto.

CHAPTER 12
TWO SIDES OF THE WIRE

Craig leaned back in his chair, watching as Kirsten paced like a caged lioness, her nails biting into the file in her hand. The air between them crackled with unspoken words, the weight of their shared past hanging heavy.

'Are you gonna say something, or are we playing the silent treatment game?' Craig finally broke the tension, his tone edged with impatience.

Kirsten stopped mid-stride, turning on her heel. 'I swear, Craig, you've gotten more annoying since your return from Italy.'

He let out a smile that dared her to react. 'And you've gotten more dramatic. What's in the file, Kirst?'

She tossed it onto his desk. 'Marco. Eddie. All of it. You need to see this.'

Craig sighed, rubbing his temples before flipping the file open. 'You know, back in the day, we were chasing carjackers and drug dealers. Now we're dealing with psychopaths playing chess with our justice system.'

Kirsten crossed her arms. 'Back in the day, we also had each other's backs. That hasn't changed.'

He glanced up, their eyes locking for a moment. Years of trust had passed between them—through being partners on the beat, enduring late-night stakeouts, surviving shootouts and lousy coffee. They knew each other's rhythms, and the unspoken language between them was stronger than words. Childhood crushes had faded, but their bond never had.

Craig was first to look away, scanning the papers. 'You're telling me Eddie and Paulo are the same guy? Where did you get this intel? I heard it from Alessandro in Italy.'

'I overheard them talking behind closed doors on my rich-bitch stakeout with Lincoln. I'm telling you, Marco's been playing us. Eddie—Paulo—is his inside man, and we must stop whatever they're planning before it's too late.'

'Damn it.' Craig pushed the folder aside. 'I turned down two promotions to stay on this case, and you're juggling two jobs to keep a spotlight on Marco. We are not letting this bastard get the upper hand.'

Kirsten nodded. 'Exactly why we need X. He's got access. If anyone can confirm what those two are up to, it's him.'

Craig picked up his phone. 'Then let's get him in play.'

* * *

X leaned against the chain-link fence, eyes scanning the yard as he lit a cigarette. Marco and Eddie stood a few feet away, their voices low, their body language cautious.

Eddie glanced toward X before shifting closer to Marco. 'These days, I don't like talking out here.'

Marco grinned, his teeth flashing. 'Relax. X is too busy playing nice with the guards. He doesn't know jack.'

X exhaled smoke, pretending not to notice the brief look Marco shot his way. He knew these two were up to something, but they weren't careless. Not with him standing there.

'You two gonna keep whispering like lovebirds, or are you

actually talking business?' X called out.

Marco chuckled. 'Wouldn't you like to know?'

Eddie flicked him a glare. 'We're just shooting the shit, man. Nothing serious.'

Shrugging, X took another drag. 'Whatever you say.' He pushed off the fence and wandered toward a group of inmates playing cards, keeping his ears open as he walked away.

The moment X was out of earshot, Eddie turned to Marco. 'Are you insane? Why even talk out here?'

A quiet chuckle curled at the edge of Marco's grin. 'Because I like watching him squirm.'

Eddie leaned in. 'We're set. Noctis has three guards on payroll, including that dick Davis. I'm still trying to wrap my head around him being dirty. I guess one never can tell these days. Anyways, they'll be on duty the night we move.'

'And if something goes wrong?'

'It won't. The guards are handling the cameras and alarms. All we have to do is get to the loading dock. From there, we're ghosts .'

Marco exhaled, his fingers twitching. 'Transportation?'

'A van will be waiting two blocks away. It'll take us straight to the docks.' Eddie shot another glance toward where X was laughing with the card players. 'You sure about this?'

Marco grabbed Eddie's collar, pulling him close. 'Have I ever been unsure?'

Eddie focused on him for a long moment before nodding. 'Fine. We do it your way.'

Marco grinned. 'That's the spirit.'

The prison bell clanged, signalling the end of yard time. Marco released Eddie with a clap on the back, his voice low and confident.

'In forty-eight hours, we're walking out of here. And no one's gonna stop us.'

From across the yard, X watched as Marco and Eddie headed inside. He flicked his cigarette to the ground, crushing it under his boot.

X sensed something was coming. And it was going to be big.

CHAPTER 13
SLIP THE CAGE

Forty-eight hours later to the minute, the prison lay shrouded in its usual oppressive silence—yet beneath the stillness, the air vibrated with anticipation. Every detail of the plan had been honed to perfection. The moment had arrived.

Marco adjusted his collar, glancing at Eddie, whose fingers drummed a rapid, silent beat against his thigh. 'Showtime,' Marco muttered. His heart hammered, but he was deadpan.

'Let's get the party started,' Eddie said with a wicked grin.

The first checkpoint was Davis. He was a raging storm in motion—thunderous, relentless, and impossible to ignore. Orders flew from his mouth like lightning bolts, and woe to anyone in his path; he'd shove inmates aside without a second thought. But tonight? As he chivvied them out of the yard, he almost looked pleasant, as much as a man with a permanent scowl could. Amazing what a little persuasion—or, in this case, an obscene amount of money—could do.

'Davis, you're looking downright cheerful tonight,' Eddie teased, barely keeping his smirk in check. 'What happened—someone slip a love note in your lunch? Or did a unicorn prance through here and grant you three wishes?'

Davis grunted, glancing around to ensure nobody had followed them down the hallway. 'Yeah, and if you don't shut up, I'll shove it down your throat.'

'That's the Davis we know and tolerate,' Marco quipped as Davis unlocked a door. 'Let's get this ballet moving.'

Marco and Eddie stepped through the door, and it clicked shut behind them, followed by the rattle of Davis locking it from the other side. The corridor beyond was empty, just as planned. But every shadow felt like a watchful eye, every distant clank of metal a harbinger of disaster. When they slipped past the first set of security cameras, McAllister's handiwork came into play—the looping footage of their empty cells ran smoothly.

'This loop better hold, Mac,' Marco murmured as they passed the surveillance room.

McAllister barely moved but gave a slow thumbs-up. 'Until the next shift change, you're ghosts.'

Ghosts. That was the plan. No alarms. No bodies. No traces.

But just as they neared the stairwell, voices echoed from below. A pair of guards, off their usual route.

'Damn it,' Eddie whispered.

Marco grabbed his arm and pulled him into a shadowed alcove. They held their breath as the two men walked past, their conversation about weekend plans utterly mundane and yet terrifying in its potential to unravel everything. One wrong step, one accidental noise, and it was over.

The moment stretched into eternity before the guards disappeared around the corner. Eddie exhaled. 'Bloody hell, that was close. I nearly swallowed my tongue.'

'Keep it together,' Marco whispered.

They moved swiftly down the stairwell, reaching the loading dock—the final hurdle. Ruiz stood near the truck, checking his watch, his foot tapping impatiently.

'You're late,' Ruiz hissed as they approached.

'Traffic was a nightmare,' Eddie shot back.

Ruiz snickered, then turned to unlock the truck. That's when a spotlight flared to life at the far end of the dock, sweeping the area.

'Not in the plan,' Marco murmured.

A second too long in the open and they were toast. Ruiz cursed under his breath. 'Plan's changed,' he said, nodding toward a row of haphazardly stacked crates. 'Get behind there. Now.'

They bolted. Marco felt the heat of the spotlight skim past as he dived behind the crates, Eddie practically landing on top of him.

'This is cosy,' Eddie muttered.

'Shut up.'

A voice crackled over a radio nearby. 'Sector Five clear. Moving on.' The spotlight swept away, plunging them back into darkness.

Ruiz gave them the signal. They sprinted for the truck. The back doors swung open just as sirens blared from the other side of the prison. A false alarm? A real one? No time to question it. Marco and Eddie lunged forward, the doors slamming behind them with a metallic clang. Their hearts pounded as they exchanged breathless glances—no turning back now.

The engine roared to life, tyres pressing hard against the pavement as the truck lurched forward, shooting out through Steelvale's gates seconds before they clashed shut. Marco pushed his back against the cold metal interior, his chest rising and falling rapidly. Eddie let out a high-pitched laugh.

'That was all too easy,' he mused, shaking his head. 'Almost makes you wonder.'

Marco bared his teeth in something that wasn't quite human. 'That's what happens when the right players are in place. Noctis owns this chessboard, and we're the pawns right now. But who says for how long!'

The truck jolted as it hit a bump in the road. Neither man flinched. They were already focused on what came next. The escape had been a masterpiece of planning, but the real fight was just beginning.

CHAPTER 14
HERE WE COME

For two nights, Marco and Eddie had lain low in a nameless safe house, a crumbling relic of a place two and a half hours north of Steelvale. The walls smelled of dust and damp wood, the floorboards groaned underfoot, and their only company was the occasional scurrying creature in the dark. It had been a necessary pause—a place to catch their breath and reassess—but the atmosphere inside had wound tighter with each passing hour. They both knew it: staying in one place was a death sentence. Flannery's reach was long, and his thirst for vengeance was deep as the grave Marco envisioned for him. So, when dawn's first light bled across the sky, they were already on the move again.

The unmarked van idled like a caged beast, its engine rumbling low as Marco and Eddie clambered inside. The doors slammed shut, sealing them in. The driver, a silent hulk of a man with a scar running down his cheek, didn't so much as glance at them. He answered only to Clutch; that was all they needed to know.

Without a word, Clutch threw the van into gear, tyres screeching as they sped off into the dying night. The city lights faded in the rearview mirror, swallowed by the vast emptiness of the countryside. Hours passed, and the only sound was the rhythmic thrum of the tyres against the road, a metronome counting down to whatever lay ahead.

Shifting uncomfortably in his seat, Eddie finally broke the

silence. 'You gonna tell me where we're going, or do I just keep pretending this is some scenic midnight joyride?'

Clutch barely spared him a glance. 'You'll see soon enough.'

Eddie exhaled sharply. 'Great. Love a good mystery.'

The van turned onto a dirt road, bumping and rattling as it carved through a landscape of dense, untamed wilderness. Eventually, the headlights illuminated their destination—a decrepit old farmhouse hunched against the landscape like a forgotten child. Paint peeled from its walls in jagged strips, and the windows were dark, hollow voids. It was miles from civilization; the perfect hideout.

Clutch killed the engine. Marco and Eddie stepped out, the crunch of gravel beneath their boots echoing in the eerie quiet.

'Charming,' Eddie said. 'Just screams 'Welcome home!"

Marco ignored him and pushed open the door. The inside wasn't much better—dust, cobwebs, and the faint smell of rot. Marco flicked on an old lamp, its glow casting jagged shadows against the walls. He turned to Eddie, wearing a mask of calm. 'You did good back there.'

'That almost sounded like a compliment. You feeling okay?'

Marco's eyes blackened. 'Don't get comfortable. This isn't over. Not even close.'

Eddie's smirk faded. He knew Marco well enough to recognize that tone. The wheels in his head were already spinning, calculating their next move.

As the sun crept toward the horizon, Marco sat by the window, staring out at the endless stretch of trees. Escape was one thing. Surviving what came next was another. Flannery wouldn't just be angry—he'd be obsessed. Marco and Eddie had shattered his control, humiliated him. That wasn't something a man like

Flannery forgave.

Marco turned as Eddie tossed a can of beans onto the rickety table. 'So, what's the plan, mastermind? We just sit here, roast marshmallows, and wait for them to come knocking?'

'No.' Marco's lips curled into a humourless smile. 'We go after Flannery first.'

Eddie blinked. 'Come again?'

Marco leaned forward, his voice cold and steady. 'Flannery isn't the type to let this go. He'll hunt us until we really *are* ghosts... unless we take him out before he gets the chance.'

Shaking his head, Eddie let out a low chuckle. 'Damn, Marco. You don't do things half-heartedly, do you?'

Marco didn't respond. His mind was already working. He predicted that Flannery would've taken a few days' leave, regrouping, holding private meetings with his inner circle. He was wounded—physically and mentally—and Marco knew he'd stop at nothing to reclaim his control. Their names would already be on the FBI's most-wanted list, plastered across every news outlet. Flannery would've made sure of that.

But he had made one critical mistake. He thought he still had control.

Marco had contacts, resources, and leverage. And, most importantly, he suspected that The Architect of Noctis wanted Flannery dead. A message on the burner phone he found in the kitchen indicated exactly where Flannery would be—his private cabin, buried deep in the woods. Isolated. Vulnerable.

But a shadow lingered in the back of Marco's mind. X was still out there, left behind in Steelvale. A wild card. An unknown variable in an otherwise perfect equation.

Marco pushed the thought aside. Flannery came first. The

warden was the biggest threat, and threats had to be eliminated.

As the sun dipped below the trees, painting the sky in streaks of red and gold, Marco spoke, his voice quiet but firm. 'We move at dawn.'

Eddie matched Marco's gaze, unwavering. 'Then let's make it count.'

The game had changed. The hunted had become the hunters. And when the dust settled, only one side would be left standing.

CHAPTER 15
THE WARDEN'S JUDGEMENT

The night pressed in, dense and airless, suffocating the moonlight that struggled to pierce the canopy of trees. Marco and Eddie crouched low behind the dense underbrush, their eyes fixed on the lone figure stepping out of the cabin. Flannery locked the door behind him with a heavy thud that echoed in the silence of the night. His stern face, weathered by decades of wielding authority, showed no awareness of the shadows lurking at the edge of his vision, following his every move, waiting for the right moment to strike.

This cabin was his sanctuary, a retreat far from the madding crowd, where he could escape the weight of his duties. The flickering candlelight inside cast a warm, inviting glow, starkly contrasting the cold reality outside. He had plans for the evening—his wife was joining him, and he envisioned a peaceful night filled with laughter and love.

But as he walked toward the shed to get more firewood, unease slithered down his spine. He brushed it off, chalking it up to the stress of recent days. Little did he know his fate had already been sealed.

Marco's hand tightened around the hilt of his knife, his knuckles white in the dim light. His pulse quickened, spurred by the familiar rush of adrenaline that came with the hunt. This was personal. The warden had humiliated him and stripped him of his dignity, and tonight, Marco would have his revenge.

Eddie, crouched beside him, was a shadow of malice, his eyes glinting with cruel anticipation. Authority figures like Flannery disgusted him, and the thought of bringing one to his knees filled Eddie with dark satisfaction. He glanced at Marco and gave a slight nod. It was time.

Flannery reached the shed, oblivious to the two figures moving silently through the darkness. They pounced simultaneously, predators who had rehearsed this moment a thousand times. Marco's knife was at Flannery's throat before he could utter a sound, and Eddie shoved a rag into his mouth, stifling any cries for help.

'Evening, Warden,' Marco hissed into his ear, voice dripping with venom. 'We've got some unfinished business.'

Flannery's eyes widened in terror as he was dragged toward the edge of the forest. He struggled, but Marco's grip was unyielding, fuelled by years of pent-up rage. Eddie followed closely, a grin spreading across his face as he watched Flannery's futile attempts to free himself. The warden had no idea what awaited him in the depths of those woods.

They moved quickly, their steps swift and practiced, until they were deep within the forest, far from prying eyes. Flannery was forced to his knees, his hands bound tightly behind his back. The trees around them stood tall and indifferent, witnesses to the cruelty that was about to unfold.

Marco circled Flannery, his knife gleaming as it caught the faint moonlight filtering through the leaves. He paused before the warden, crouching down so their faces were inches apart.

'You remember me? The one that got away?' Marco whispered. Flannery's eyes flickered, and Marco's lips curled into a wicked smile. 'I didn't think we'd catch up so quickly; you must have really missed me and my wicked sense of humour. *Wicked* being the operative word, huh, Flannery?'

Eddie leaned against a nearby tree, arms crossed, watching the scene with dark amusement. 'He's all yours, Marco,' he said lazily. 'Show him what happens when you mess with the wrong people.'

Marco didn't need any encouragement. The blade of his knife traced a slow, deliberate line across Flannery's cheek, drawing a thin ribbon of blood. Flannery winced, his body trembling as fear took hold. Marco's eyes burned with a cold fury, fuelled by the memories of every insult and slight. 'You took everything from me,' he snarled, his voice growing louder, more unhinged. 'But now it's my turn.'

What followed was an hour of sheer torment. The gag muffled Flannery's screams, his pleas for mercy falling on deaf ears. Marco was meticulous. Each cut calculated to inflict maximum pain without ending the man's life too quickly. Eddie watched, occasionally offering a suggestion or a taunt, his enjoyment growing with every drop of blood spilled.

When Flannery's strength finally waned, Marco looked to Eddie. The two locked eyes, a silent understanding passing between them. Marco stepped back, breathing heavily, his hands stained with Flannery's blood.

'Your turn,' he said, handing the knife to Eddie.

Eddie took it with a grin. He paced around Flannery, savouring the moment. The warden was barely conscious, his head lolling forward as he fought to remain upright. But Eddie wasn't done with him yet. He knelt beside Flannery, whispering in his ear, his voice soft but deadly. 'You should've known better. Men like us... we're not to be trifled with.'

With a swift, practiced motion, Eddie drove the knife into Flannery's chest, twisting it slowly. His body jerked, eyes wide with pain and fear as the life drained out of him. When he finally went still, Eddie stood, wiping the blade on the dead man's shirt. He turned to Marco, a satisfied smile on his lips. 'You've got a real talent,' he said. 'Precise, clean strokes, just enough to keep them alive until the end. You'd make a fine surgeon... or butcher.'

Marco gave a grim chuckle, the tension in his body slowly dissipating. He looked down at Flannery's lifeless body. 'You're not so bad yourself,' he replied.

They stood silently for a moment, the reality of what they'd done sinking in. But there was no guilt, no remorse; only a shared exhilaration, a wicked satisfaction, a bond forged in blood. This was who they were—predators, hunters, two sides of the same dark coin.

Marco pulled out the burner phone and sent a message.

It's done.

As they walked away from the warden's shallow grave, the darkness swallowed them whole, leaving no trace of the horrors they had wrought. Flannery's time was over, but the night was still young for Marco and Eddie. And there were so many more lives left to claim.

Their twisted bond was stronger than ever, and their thirst for blood was insatiable. They were a force of nature, unstoppable and relentless, and they would leave no survivors.

CHAPTER 16
SHADOWS AND DECEIT

The low hum of the city echoed through the night. Kirsten adjusted the collar of her leather jacket as she stepped out of the cab, into the dimly lit parking lot, her heels clicking sharply against the wet pavement. She wasn't here for pleasantries. She was here to talk to the cabal's top dog—the man who ran the show—not these wannabes she'd been wasting time with. She had no patience left for games.

The frigid night air stung her face but didn't deter her. 'How much longer?' she muttered, her voice tight, as she checked her watch. The agent with her, a tall, dark-haired man with a scar above his lip, gave her a wry smile. His role was simple—keep her covered and make sure nothing went sideways. He was a part of Craig's operation, one of the best. But tonight, their tension was palpable. They both knew they were about to walk into a den of snakes.

'Don't worry, Kirsten. We'll get what we need.'

She eyed him but said nothing. She wasn't sure she believed in the system anymore. For weeks, she had been chasing leads, spinning her wheels with low-level players, getting nowhere. Finally, now, thanks to a hint from Alessandro's network and her own relentless demands for a meeting, she was minutes from confronting the big fish.

When her phone buzzed with a blank message from a blocked number, she walked briskly through the dimly lit alley toward the unmarked door. It was barely noticeable, tucked between two nondescript buildings, as if trying to stay out of sight.

Inside, the club was a maze of shadows and smoke. The heavy bass of some forgotten song vibrated through the walls, but there was little cheer in the air. A couple of lowlifes hunched over the bar, their murmurs drowned by the music. Dim lighting barely illuminated the room, casting long shadows that seemed to whisper secrets. The place smelled like stale alcohol and faded desperation. This wasn't her scene and wasn't where she wanted to be.

They followed the doorman, a giant with a gold earring and a permanent scowl, to a narrow hallway. They passed several rooms that leaked muffled laughter and clinking glasses before stopping at a nondescript door.

The door creaked open, and they stepped into a sparse office. Slick, the cabal's lackey and middleman, greeted them with a nod. His greasy hair hung limply by his ears, and his crooked smile seemed more forced than usual. He pushed open a door that blended into the grey walls and led them down another hallway, past a flickering lightbulb, to a small, dingy room in the back. Its heavy red velvet curtains were drawn tight, blocking any semblance of life outside. A cheap fake floral arrangement sat on the bar counter, its colours faded and forgotten. The furniture was worn, mismatched; old, beat-up bar stools lined the space, their crimson cushions looking like they'd seen better days decades ago.

Charming! Kirsten thought sarcastically. *I need to get this over with. I can't get out of here quickly enough. This place is a joke.*

As she stepped into the room, she turned to the agent beside her, raising an eyebrow. They knew what was at stake, and both had played the game long enough to understand it wouldn't be easy.

Shuffling in after them, Slick gestured to the far side of the space, where a tall, dark partition loomed. His nervous energy seeped into the atmosphere. 'He said he'd talk to you, but not face-to-face. He's behind that screen. And, uh... his voice has been altered. Are you happy with that?'

Kirsten shot him a sharp look. 'You said we'd meet him face-to-face.'

Slick scratched the back of his neck awkwardly, a flicker of guilt in his eyes. 'Boss's orders. You don't get to set the rules, sweetheart.'

Kirsten's jaw was a vice, clamped shut around words she wouldn't let out, patience running thin, but she masked her annoyance. 'Yeah, it's not ideal, but I'll take it. Let's get this over with.' She took a seat in front of the screen, the agent positioned slightly behind her, his hand hovering near the concealed wire in his jacket.

She could feel her pulse quickening as the silence stretched on, broken only by the faint whisper of a pen against paper. From the corner of her eye, she noticed a man sitting in the shadows near the back, scribbling notes—likely a bodyguard or confidant. His eyes never left her, and his gaze was sharp. It made her uneasy.

Finally, a voice—a low whisper—came from behind the screen.

'Ms Wells, it's a pleasure. I am The Architect. I trust you've enjoyed the ambiance?' The voice was smooth, like honey, but something was unsettling about it. 'I hear you've been looking for me. I must admit, I've been watching you.'

Kirsten's stomach clenched. She didn't like the way he said her name. 'Cut the crap,' she snapped. 'I need answers, and I need them now. Marco and Eddie are on the run. Champaign PD's been in overdrive, and the US Marshals are involved.'

The Architect's voice crackled slightly, as though he were deliberately masking his tone. 'Oh, I've heard. Quite a mess, isn't it?' His words carried a sense of satisfaction. 'But helping you?

That's a different story. You see, helping you means making a lot of noise, and, well... noise draws attention. The problem with you, Ms Wells, is that you're too focused on the chase.'

'I'm focused on finding Marco and Eddie,' she shot back, trying to keep her voice steady despite her mounting frustration. 'We both know what's important right now.'

A short pause, then The Architect's voice took on a mockingly sympathetic edge. 'Right, of course. But I'm afraid you're looking in the wrong direction. You're chasing ghosts in the wind.'

'I know what you're doing,' Kirsten snapped, her voice hardening. 'You're trying to cover for them.'

His chuckle, though distorted, sent a chill down her spine. 'I'm not covering for anyone. But look, I've got something for you. There's a place, an old warehouse on the outskirts of Springfield. That's their next stop. It's all in the details if you know how to read them.'

She didn't trust him, not one bit. But she had no choice. This was the only lead she had, despite her sinking feeling that it would just be another pointless pursuit. 'Give me the address.'

Another low laugh from behind the screen. 'I can't be that generous. But if you follow the trail from there, you'll get your answers. Just don't go in too fast, or you'll scare them off. You've got to be clever, Ms Wells. The wrong move, and everything will fall apart.'

There was another pause, and The Architect spoke again, this time with a different tone—more sinister, almost rehearsed. 'What you don't understand, Ms Wells, is that the more you chase them, the more obvious you make it they're alive. My associates are not fond of loose ends. So... I suggest you reconsider your approach. It's not the right time.'

Kirsten's anger burned brighter. This was a stall. He was playing her, feeding her a story while Marco and Eddie were likely slipping further away.

'You're sending me on a wild goose chase,' she said coldly, her eyes narrowing. 'You're stalling.'

The Architect sighed, almost as though he had expected her to catch on. 'I don't appreciate being accused of such things. I'm simply trying to help. But you're right—there's a chance that what you're asking for is... premature.'

His words echoed in the room, and momentarily, she thought she saw something move in the corner of her eye. A shadow, perhaps—or someone else here, hidden. She couldn't be sure.

She gritted her teeth. 'You're wasting my time.'

'No,' he replied, his tone now playful. 'I'm giving you a chance. Take it or leave it. But don't forget—I've had my eyes on you, just like you've had yours on me.'

Kirsten stood up abruptly, the agent following her lead. 'This isn't over,' she muttered, though she wasn't sure who she was speaking to. She turned on her heel and walked toward the door, her mind racing. The warehouse. It had to be a trap.

Behind her, The Architect's voice was the last thing she heard before the door slammed shut.

'Good luck, Ms Wells. You'll need it.'

As she stepped back into the darkness of the alley, Kirsten's mind was already working overtime. She didn't trust that man, not for a second. But if she ran out of other options, she'd have no choice but to follow his lead. Marco and Eddie were out there, and she would do whatever it took to find them—even walking straight into a lion's den.

What The Architect didn't know was that she wasn't the only one with a plan.

CHAPTER 17
A SYMPHONY OF VENGEANCE

The stench of death smothered the house like a rot-soaked cloth, but they revelled in it, their minds twisted with the thirst for more. Marco's eyes gleamed with a dark satisfaction as he studied the knife, its blade and his hands still stained with the warden's blood. 'We're just getting started,' he said, his voice low and cold.

A wicked smile stretched across Eddie's face. 'I'm with you, brother. This world doesn't stand a chance.'

'There's unfinished business in Champaign. A lot of people who've forgotten just how much they owe me.' Marco's expression turned venomous. 'And we'll start with Chad.'

'Chad? The clown from your old drama days?'

'The very one,' Marco sneered. 'Leigh's useless boyfriend. Always thought he was above everyone, including me. Smug bastard never saw what was happening right under his nose.'

Eddie chuckled darkly. 'I remember you mentioning him. Thought you let that go.'

'Oh, no.' Marco's eyes narrowed with a sinister gleam. 'Chad deserves what's coming. He was always a fool, thinking he could outshine me. But he didn't know that while he was rehearsing his weak performances, Leigh and I were flirting, and one day we'd have our own... private rehearsals.'

Eddie's eyes lit up with interest, sensing the sadistic joy his friend was taking in this. 'You and Leigh? That must have stung him.'

'Not enough came out in the court case,' Marco said, his voice dripping with mockery. 'I'll make sure to enlighten him of every intimate detail before I end his miserable existence. Every time she called out my name, every secret touch, every stolen moment. He'll hear it all.'

Marco's mind danced with the possibilities. He could already see Chad's face twisting in rage and pain as he recounted each sordid detail. The thought made his blood sing with anticipation.

'And once I'm done with him...' Marco paused, savouring the thought. 'There's more. Plenty more. We're going to turn Champaign into a graveyard.'

Eddie's excitement mirrored Marco's. He had always been up for violence, but this—this was personal. This was the kind of twisted chaos he lived for. 'I like it. But who's next after Chad?'

Marco's face turned cold as stone, his voice a whisper of malice. 'After that, we take down Alessandro Cantrello, Gabriella's pathetic brother who, in my final moments of freedom, thought a pocketknife could take me down. What a piece of work!'

'And after that?'

There was no warmth in Marco's smile; only darkness. 'Then it's Kirsten's turn. I'll make her regret every lie she reported, every promise she made to Craig. She will pay the price. And finally... Craig. Yes, Craig, the one and only, the relentless detective who humiliated me. The very one who ensured my downfall. This is a case of saving the best 'til last.'

Eddie nodded, adrenaline coursing through him. 'You never cease to amaze me. But this is all about you. What about something for me?'

'You do whatever you want. Who's gonna stop you? Start making your list, bro.' Marco snickered. 'But just remember we're on borrowed time, here. The Architect has business for us to attend to.'

* * *

The night was teeming with shadows, and Marco and Eddie moved through it like wraiths. Their minds were set on bloodshed, their hearts black with hatred. Every step was calculated, every breath a promise of violence. Champaign was not ready for the storm that was coming. Marco's rage had festered for years, and now, it was ready to explode. They were no longer just men—they were forces of destruction, and nothing would stand in their way.

As they neared Chad's house, Marco halted, inhaling deeply as if savouring the scent of vengeance. His lips curled into a predatory grin. 'It's time to remind these bastards who I am.'

Eddie cracked his knuckles, the sound sharp in the silence. 'Let's make them bleed.'

Fortune played its hand in their favour. The door was unlocked—foolish. Too trusting. A gift, really. They slipped inside, the darkness swallowing them whole. Laughter drifted from the living room, easy, unguarded. Chad and his friends had no idea death was standing in the doorway, watching, waiting.

Marco leaned into Eddie's ear, his voice a sinister whisper. 'Let's put on a show.'

Chad was sprawled on the couch, a beer in hand, laughing at something on the TV. To his right, his friend Darren was scrolling through his phone, oblivious. His mates Michelle and Blake sat nearby, deep in conversation, their drinks untouched. They were relaxed and safe—until now.

Marco stepped forward, letting his presence be known. The room froze.

Chad's face drained of colour, his mouth opening, but no words came out. His body locked up in shock. Finally, he sputtered, 'You... you're supposed to be in prison.'

Marco tilted his head slowly, deliberately, his grin widening. 'Surprise.'

Chad scrambled backward, his beer crashing to the floor. His friends jumped up, fear crackling through the air like static.

Eddie moved fast, blocking the doorway. 'Nobody's leaving.'

Chad's breath came in short gasps. 'Listen, Marco—'

'Shut up.' Marco's voice was icy, slicing through the room. He took a step forward, his eyes boring into Chad's. 'I rotted in a cage while you kept on living your pathetic little life. You thought I'd just disappear?' He let out a dark chuckle. 'No, Chad. I've been thinking about this moment for a long, long time.'

Blake lunged for his phone, but Eddie was faster. The knife flashed, and Blake screamed, clutching his bleeding hand. The phone clattered to the floor.

Marco turned back to Chad, who was trembling. 'You always thought you were safe, didn't you? Thought you could wipe your hands clean, pretend you had nothing to do with my incarceration?' He leaned closer, his voice dropping to a whisper. 'But you did, Chad. You were complicit. You all were.'

Chad tried to stand, but Marco grabbed him by the throat, shoving him against the wall. 'You sold me out with your testimony,' Marco hissed. 'You let them take me.'

Gasping, Chad clawed at Marco's hand, his face turning red. 'I-I didn't—'

Marco tightened his grip. 'Don't lie to me.'

Darren charged forward, but Eddie intercepted, driving his knife into Darren's gut. Darren staggered, a gurgling sound escaping his lips as blood seeped through his shirt. He collapsed, twitching violently. Michelle screamed, bolting toward the hallway. Eddie caught her ponytail, yanking her back with such force she fell to the floor, sobbing.

Marco grinned at Chad, savouring the terror in his eyes. 'I could kill you right now,' Marco murmured, 'but where's the fun in that?'

He released Chad, only to drive a brutal punch into his stomach. Chad doubled over, wheezing. Marco grabbed him by the hair, dragging his head back. 'You're going to die, Chad. But not quickly.'

He slammed Chad's face into the coffee table. Bone crunched. Blood splattered across the wood. Chad screamed, writhing in agony.

Marco crouched beside him, his voice a mockery of sympathy. 'Leigh told me everything, you know. The way you strung her along, the lies, the cheating. And while you were off playing games, she found refuge in my arms.'

Chad's bloody face twisted in horror. 'You're lying.'

Marco chuckled. 'Oh, no. We all know why she came home.' He leaned in close. 'I know exactly how she tasted. I know the sounds she made. And I know she wished she had chosen me all along.' Chad let out a strangled growl, weakly trying to push Marco away, but it only made him laugh louder. 'That's right. While you were busy being the town's gigolo, she was in my bed.'

Rage flickered in Chad's eyes, but he was too broken to fight back. Marco relished his suffering. 'That's the last thing you'll think about, Chad. Every kiss. Every whisper. Every moment she gave to me instead of you.'

Eddie chuckled, enjoying the chaos. He turned to Michelle and

Blake, his knife glinting. 'We can do this the easy way or the hard way.'

Blake bolted for the door. Eddie threw the knife. It hit its mark. Blake collapsed, choking on his own blood.

Michelle was sobbing, still on the floor, her hands raised in surrender. 'Please... please don't.'

Marco wasn't listening. He turned from Chad, grabbing a poker from the fireplace. 'This is for every day I spent in that hellhole.'

The poker came down hard. Again. And again. Chad's screams echoed through the house, raw and unholy. Marco didn't stop. He couldn't. The rage and the years of torment poured out in every swing. When he finally stepped back, Chad was nothing but a broken, bloodied husk.

Marco exhaled, his chest heaving. He turned to Michelle, whose body shook with terror. He knelt beside her, lifting her chin with the bloodied poker. 'You're going to send a message for me.'

She whimpered, nodding frantically.

Marco grinned. 'Tell them... Marco is back.'

With that, he stood, motioning for Eddie. 'We're done here.'

Eddie wiped his knife clean on Blake's shirt and followed Marco to the door. The night greeted them, cool and indifferent, and they disappeared into it, leaving behind a house of horrors.

CHAPTER 18
PORTRAIT OF PAIN

As Marco and Eddie sped through the dimly lit streets in a stolen car, energy crackled between them, a shared exhilaration for the destruction they had already caused and the chaos still ahead. The city of Champaign had no idea what was coming.

'The Cantrellos are next,' Marco muttered, eyes narrowing as he thought about what awaited them. 'I've got unfinished business there.'

Eddie chortled, glancing over. 'More of your 'old friends'? You've got a lot of people to settle scores with.'

Marco laughed darkly. 'You have no idea. This one's personal. It's not just about blood; it's about history.'

They pulled up to the Cantrellos' house. The tall, stately building looming in the night, as lifeless as the quiet street it sat on. There were no lights lit within. No movement. Marco stared at it, rage bubbling up again.

'What the fuck?' he fumed. 'It looks like nobody's home!'

'Maybe they've been expecting trouble,' Eddie said, leaning forward and scanning the place. 'All locked up, no sign of life.'

'They can't hide,' Marco growled, stepping out of the car, his boots crunching on the gravel. 'Nobody can.'

He splintered the front door with a quick, forceful kick, sending it crashing inward, the bang echoing through the darkened house like a death knell. There was no plan—just destruction.

As Marco made his way through the house, memories flooded back. He stopped at the entrance to the living room, staring at the couch. He could see himself sitting there all those years ago, waiting. Waiting for Gabriella.

For a fleeting moment, a smile played on his lips. How simple it had all seemed back then. But then his eyes travelled up to the large painting hanging above the fireplace—a magnificent portrait of Gabriella.

His expression darkened. Rage boiled inside him, raw and untamed. He stalked over to the fireplace and tore the portrait from the wall, gripping the edges so hard the canvas buckled. With a roar, he threw it to the ground and stomped on it, over and over, until the frame was shattered, and the canvas was a crumpled mess beneath his boots.

'I'm so glad I got rid of you, you little bitch!' Marco screamed, his voice hoarse with rage. His fists clenched as he paced in front of the ruined portrait. 'You knew how much I liked you when you were my student. God, how many times did I hint at it? How many times did I try to get you to understand?'

He kicked the remains of the portrait, breathing heavily, his eyes wild. 'But no, the little goody two-shoes wouldn't take the hint. So, you ended up on the Chesterfield. Why the hell did I give you that last piece of dignity? You didn't deserve it. I should've dragged you up those stairs and left you there. But whatever... I got my revenge, didn't I? And now...' He grinned viciously. 'Now it's your brothers' turn. Especially that little prick Alessandro.' Marco's voice dropped to a sneer. 'He thought he could scare me with a pocketknife. Like that would have done much damage, really! Can't wait to get my hands on him.'

As Marco stood seething over the destroyed portrait, Eddie

strolled into the room, his eyes wide with delight. 'Jeezus, you never told me these assholes were so loaded!' he shrieked, practically bouncing with excitement. He had a handful of watches, gold chains, diamond rings, and antique cufflinks. 'Look at this haul!' He twirled around, giddy. 'It would've taken months to rack up this much back home. I'm stoked!'

Marco barely glanced at the treasures in Eddie's grip. 'Yeah,' he muttered. 'Nice.'

Eddie stopped dancing and tilted his head toward the portrait, his grin fading slightly. 'Who's that?' he asked.

Marco's voice was cold, devoid of any emotion. 'The great Gabriella Cantrello. She looks better this way—tattered and torn.'

Eddie let out a low whistle. 'Well, my man, I've gotta hand it to you. You sure do have taste when it comes to the fairer sex.' He snickered, eyeing the ruined portrait with mild interest. Then his tone shifted, his eyes twinkling with mischief. 'Speaking of, what was that other bitch's name you mentioned on the way here? The one you've got plans for?'

Marco glanced at him, his dark expression lifting slightly, a cruel smile creeping onto his face. 'That would be Kirsten,' he said. 'But don't worry, we'll get to her. Right now, we've got Alessandro to track down. He's next.'

Eddie's grin returned, full of excitement. 'Hell yeah.'

Then, together, they moved like a storm through the grand living room, overturning furniture with reckless force. Marco swiped his arm across a glass cabinet, sending crystal vases and delicate figurines shattering to the floor.

'Damn,' Eddie marvelled. 'These people love their fancy shit.' He picked up a framed family photo and studied it for a moment, then spat on the glass and chucked it across the room. It shattered against the wall, shards scattering over the plush carpet.

Marco smiled without warmth—predatory, deliberate. 'Not anymore.' He grabbed an ornate lamp, its base carved with gold filigree, and hurled it through the massive bay window. The glass exploded outward, raining onto the pristine flower beds outside.

Eddie, grinning wildly, snatched up a heavy iron poker from the fireplace and drove it through the television screen. Sparks crackled as the screen caved inward with a satisfying crunch. 'That's for broadcasting garbage,' he sneered.

They worked in a frenzy, their destruction ruthless, tearing apart everything that reeked of wealth and status. Family portraits were slashed with a hunting knife, the smiles defaced with deep, jagged cuts. Marco overturned a liquor cabinet, sending expensive bottles crashing to the carpet, soaking into the fibres. The pungent scent of whiskey thickened the air. 'Such a waste,' he mocked, kicking the shards aside.

Upstairs, the carnage continued. Marco yanked open a closet, pulling expensive suits off their hangers and tossing them to Eddie, who slashed through the fabric with his knife. 'Think old man Cantrello's gonna show up to his fancy meetings in rags now?' Eddie laughed.

Marco grabbed a handful of pearl necklaces from a jewellery box and crushed them under his boot. 'Nah, he won't be showing up anywhere for a while.' He pulled out a cigarette, took a slow drag, then flicked the burning tip onto the silk sheets of the master bed, leaving a smouldering hole.

Not wanting to be left out of anything, Eddie emptied an entire bottle of cologne over the closet before tossing in a lit match, the flames licking up in greedy hunger.

They stood in the centre of the wreckage, taking it all in. The house was a war zone of broken glass, ruined furniture, and acrid smoke. Their reign of terror was well and truly underway. The power, the control—it was intoxicating. The city would tremble under their grip before they were done.

Eddie reached into his pocket and pulled out a crumpled, stained list, scanning the scribbled names. He grinned. 'The Cantrellos are done,' he muttered, dragging a thick black line through the name. 'Second one down, and many more to go!'

Marco took the list, his eyes flickering over the remaining names. It wasn't getting shorter. If anything, it was growing. The city would learn—one by one, they would all pay.

He handed the list back to Eddie. 'Now... Alessandro.'

Eddie cracked his knuckles, his grin widening. 'Let's go say hello.'

Marco flicked his cigarette onto the liquor-soaked carpet, watching the ember sizzle before stomping it out with his boot. 'Yeah,' he said, heading for the door. 'But first we gotta find the prick, and then we make it memorable.'

The stench of old cigarettes and cheap bourbon sharpened the air of the dark, dusty basement, mixing with the sounds of muffled laughter and whispers from the Noctis lowlifes scattered around the room. Marco and Eddie were comfortable here. Among like-minded friends, they could let their guard down for a moment, basking in the knowledge that they had escaped.

But as much as Marco revelled in his newfound freedom, his mind was consumed with one thing:

Alessandro.

'So,' Eddie said, slouching back in his chair, puffing on his smoke, 'you reckon this Al bloke's really that tough to track down? Don't make me laugh—we've bagged harder mugs than him, easy.'

Marco, sitting across from him with his arms crossed, glared. 'It's not that simple. The little shit has disappeared completely. And I need him found.'

Eddie chuckled, exhaling smoke through his nose. 'You're obsessed, man. You want him that bad?'

Shadows crept across Marco's face as his fingers drummed a slow, deliberate rhythm on the table. 'Alessandro was always a coward—clinging to stronger men, whispering lies behind my back. Especially to Gabriella. They were tight. Too tight. And I know the kind of poison they spread.' His lip curled. 'I should've taken care of him years ago. But the moment that sealed it was when I was being dragged out of that courtroom in cuffs, and he ran up to me—with a pathetic little knife—and said he was going to bring me down.' Marco's fist slammed the table, the sound sharp and final. 'That was his mistake. Now, it's my turn.'

Eddie raised an eyebrow, looking amused. 'So where do we start?'

'We find everyone who knows him. He couldn't have gone too far.' Marco stood up, pacing around the room, eyes scanning the other faces in the club. 'I need names. Locations. Whoever knows where he is—round them up.'

'Man, you're not playing around.'

'Not with this one,' Marco said, eyes narrowing. 'Not with him.'

* * *

Later that night, they called a gathering of their most trusted contacts in Noctis—old faces they could rely on for information. There was Steve, a low-level thug who knew everyone, including the law-abiding citizens. Lucy had her ear to every dirty deal happening in town. Then there was Tyler, a hacker who could find just about anything—or anyone—with the right incentive.

Marco leaned against the back wall, watching as the tiny motel room filled up. The tension thickened as the members gathered. He exchanged a look with Eddie before stepping forward.

'All right, listen up,' Marco began, his voice commanding the room. 'We've got a target. Alessandro bloody Cantrello. You know the name. You know the history. I need every bit of intel you can get.'

Lucy spoke up first, her eyes glinting with curiosity. 'You think he's still around here? He hasn't been seen since your trial.'

Eddie laughed from his corner, shaking his head. 'No, sweetheart. He'd be smarter than that. But we're even smarter. Ain't that right,

Marco?'

Marco nodded. 'Word on the street is he left town, maybe even the country.'

Tyler, hunched over his laptop, grunted. 'If he left the country, it won't be easy to track him down. Airports, customs… every move's being watched. You two make the news every damn night.'

'Which is why we have to be smart,' Marco snapped. 'He's hiding, but not in plain sight. He's probably gone back to Italy. That's what we need to find out.'

Standing in the corner with his foot on the table, one corner of his mouth lifted, almost involuntarily, Steve retorted. 'I know some people who can poke around. Get us some tips. But, you know, nothing's free.'

Marco rolled his eyes. 'You'll get what you deserve, Steve. Just find him.'

For the next hour, the room buzzed with whispers, leads, and speculations. Steve had contacts in Europe, a thief called Teresina had family in Malta, and Tyler was already hacking into databases, looking for anything unusual under Alessandro's name.

Then, with one electrifying phone call from across the ocean, the truth was confirmed—Alessandro was back in Italy. But this wasn't just a visit or a temporary move. He had returned with purpose, stepping into the ranks of the Italian police force.

Finally, after sorting through all the information, paying what they needed to, and dismissing the gathering, Marco and Eddie sat in the back corner of the room, reviewing what they had.

Eddie let out a heavy sigh. 'Getting there? Now *that's* the real problem.'

Marco's knuckles whitened as he balled his fists. 'We can't leave the country without setting off alarms. We're stuck here.'

'So, what now?' Eddie asked. 'We let this one go?'

Marco's eyes flashed with a deadly calm. 'No. We put him on ice—for now. He'll be dealt with eventually. But first...' His lips curled into a slow, sinister grin. 'We focus on Kirsten.'

'The know-it-all journalist?'

Marco nodded, his grin widening. 'Yeah. That little bitch thought she could ruin me with her lies. She sat behind her keyboard, writing hit pieces like she actually knew something. Like she had the right to judge me.' His voice darkened, dripping with malice. 'She painted me as some kind of monster. But she was wrong.' He leaned forward, his voice dropping to a whisper. 'She hasn't even seen the half of it.'

A quiet chuckle curled at the edge of Eddie's grin, shaking his head. 'I like the sound of that. What's the plan?'

Marco sat back, tapping his fingers on the table. 'First, we take her. No one just disappears anymore, Eddie. People always leave traces—unless you know how to do it right.' His eyes gleamed. 'I want her to beg. To scream. And then, when she finally understands what real fear is...' He exhaled slowly, savouring the thought. 'Then I'll decide what happens next.'

Eddie chuckled. 'And then there's Craig.'

At the mention of the name, Marco's entire demeanour shifted. His jaw tightened; his nails dug into the table. Craig. The detective. The one who put him behind bars. The man who thought he had won.

'Craig Ryan ruined everything,' Marco growled, his voice filled with venom. 'Tracked me. Played hero. He thought he was so damn clever.' The table cracked as he gripped it tighter. 'But he has no idea what's coming for him.'

Eddie's amusement was unwavering. 'So, what do we do about him?'

Marco exhaled sharply, forcing himself to calm down. Then, a wicked smile spread across his face. 'We take our time. But before we even touch him, we go for Chelsea.'

'Chelsea? Craig's daughter?'

'She's young. Naïve. She'll be easy to manipulate. We get close, and when the time's right...' Marco let the words hang in the air, his grin deepening. 'We take her. Imagine Craig's face when he realizes his perfect little girl is gone. Imagine how fast he'll crumble when he knows it's his fault.'

Eddie gave a quiet, impressed whistle. 'Damn, Marco. That's cold—even for you.'

'I learned patience in that cell, Eddie. Craig doesn't get a quick death. No. I want him to feel it. Every. Single. Second.'

Eddie grinned. 'The world has missed your special brand of chaos.'

Marco wore the look of someone already winning, rising from his seat. 'It's good to be free, Eddie. Now it's time we act.'

They stood together, the street below them buzzing with oblivious passersby. Their next targets were set.

Alessandro could wait. But somewhere in the city, completely unaware... Kirsten was already running out of time.

CHAPTER 20
BLOOD ON THE HORIZON

Café Kopi buzzed with conversation, but Craig couldn't focus on any of it. He sat across from Kirsten, his fingers tapping against his coffee cup, drawn tight with tension.

'I still can't really believe that piece of shit managed to escape from Steelvale,' Craig muttered, rubbing his temples.

'What does it mean for us, Craig?' Kirsten asked. There was a deepening fear in her expression, one she couldn't mask no matter how hard she tried.

Craig leaned back in his chair, exhaling heavily. 'God only knows, Kirst. Steelvale is supposed to be impenetrable. No one's ever succeeded in escaping from there.'

Kirsten bit her lip. 'And the warden... Carrera took him out.'

'Word is, he didn't just take him out—he butchered him,' Craig replied grimly. 'Marco made it brutal. Made a damn statement. That's what worries me.'

Kirsten's hand trembled as she lifted her coffee, barely managing a sip. 'We know Carrera. We've seen what he's capable of. But this Eddie... what do we actually *know* about him?'

'Only thing we've got is he used to be a Mafia hitman who went by Paulo. No photos. Just whispers. That's it. Now, ain't that just dandy?'

Kirsten's stomach twisted. She'd spent years chasing Marco, exposing every last horror, every sordid detail. But this? This felt like stepping into pitch-black water without knowing what was beneath the surface. 'So, what the hell do we do now?'

'We need more info. Fast,' Craig said, standing up and grabbing his coat. 'I'm heading to Steelvale to get a firsthand account. Whatever happened, it was planned, and more than likely an inside job. We need to figure out how deep this goes.'

Kirsten stood with him, determination replacing the fear in her eyes. 'I'll keep digging on my end. Talk to sources, anyone who might know something about Eddie. I'm not sitting on the sidelines for this one.'

'You never do! Just be careful. They'll come after you next if they know we're onto them.'

Kirsten nodded, her mind already a step ahead. 'I've dealt with worse.'

They left the café to find that the sky had darkened, hanging over them like Marco and Eddie's looming threat.

* * *

Steelvale Prison was a fortress, or so it had seemed. When Craig arrived, the scene outside was chaotic—police cars, reporters, and officials swarmed the entrance. He flashed his badge, pushing through the crowd, determined to get answers.

Acting Warden Chandy Clanwell marched into the staff briefing room like a thunderclap—unflinching, unyielding, and utterly unmissable. Her presence alone could silence a cell block. Known across the country as the woman who broke three prison riots with nothing but her voice and a glare, Clanwell had earned a fearsome reputation among inmates and officers alike. She didn't bluff, didn't bargain, and didn't back down. Steel-eyed and sharp-tongued, she was a master of control, commanding respect without ever needing to ask for it. There wasn't a man, woman, or monster behind bars who could rattle her, and those foolish enough to try quickly learned the price of underestimating the most formidable warden in the system.

They'd crossed paths once before—names, ranks, nothing more. Now, under brutal circumstances, it was different. Clanwell stood rigid, her usual iron composure strained, shock flickering across her otherwise impenetrable face. 'Lieutenant Ryan, over here!' she barked, her voice cutting through the tension like a whip crack as she waved him over. Craig moved toward her, each step slicing through the thick, rancid air, the stench of discontent hanging like smoke after a fire.

Steelvale had been breached, and it looked like the CIA HQ. 'Jesus...' he muttered, taking it all in.

'Flannery didn't stand a chance,' Clanwell said, shaking her head. 'They caught him off guard, slit his throat, and stabbed him multiple times. But they didn't stop there. They... they mutilated him. We found his body in a shallow grave close to his cabin.'

Anger bubbled inside Craig like a toxic chemical. 'How did they slip the net?'

'This wasn't some random breakout—they had help. We suspect they had people on the inside.'

Craig's eyes narrowed. 'Do you have a list of everyone on staff that night?'

Clanwell nodded, handing over a clipboard. 'We're interviewing them all, but no one saw anything suspicious. It's like the bastards vanished into thin air.'

Craig scanned the list, his mind already working through the possibilities.

Clanwell hesitated. 'There's something else...'

Craig looked up, eyebrows raised.

'They left a message.'

Clanwell showed him a photograph of the warden's cabin, where the words *'Who's Next?'* were scrawled in blood across the wall.

Craig shot out of his chair, jabbing a finger at the air as if Carrera himself were standing there. 'Of course he did! This is textbook Carrera. Same bloody play, different bloody day.' He let out a sharp, bitter laugh, gripping his hair in frustration. 'Guy's got a PhD in manipulation and a master's in predictable mayhem. And we keep falling for it.'

He turned to the others, eyes blazing.

'Well, not this time.'

* * *

Back in Champaign, Kirsten was working her own angles. She was glued to her phone, calling every contact she had. She knew people in low places and wasn't afraid to use them. Finally, she tracked down an ex-con named Jimmy through an old contact in Vice— someone who owed her more than one favour. She wasn't even sure he'd show. But he did, just after midnight, slipping into the booth across from her at a greasy diner on the edge of town. The kind of place with flickering lights, cracked vinyl seats, and a waitress who knew better than to ask questions.

Jimmy looked older than she remembered from the files—lined face, sunken eyes, hair gone salt-and-pepper. He had a twitchy edge, like he was always listening for footsteps behind him.

'You're a long way from the newsroom,' he said, glancing over his shoulder. 'You sure this is worth it?'

'I need to know about Eddie,' Kirsten said, leaning in. 'You ran with Marco. You'd know if this guy's as dangerous as he sounds.'

Jimmy scoffed. 'Dangerous? You're askin' the wrong question.' He pulled a crumpled pack of cigarettes from his jacket, tapped one out, and lit it with shaky fingers. 'You should be askin' what happens when you put a psycho and a ghost in the same room.'

He paused, eyes narrowing. 'I was with Marco when it all started—late nineties. He wasn't a boss man back then, just muscle. But mean as hell. Cold, too. The kinda guy who'd smile while breakin' your fingers. I did some runs with him—collections, intimidation gigs, a few cleanup jobs I don't care to relive. But even back then, there were stories about Eddie.'

Kirsten stayed silent, letting him talk.

'Eddie was different. Quiet. Never showed up unless someone needed disappearing. No trace, no mess, no noise. I never met him—just heard the name whispered through guys who didn't scare easy. When Marco started his spree, went totally off the rails... Eddie vanished. People thought he was dead, or maybe just done. But if he's back? And teamed up with Marco again?'

Jimmy leaned across the table, voice low and urgent. 'You're not dealin' with thugs. You're lookin' at two predators who've been off the leash too long. If they're together, something big's comin'. And it ain't gonna end pretty. Marco wouldn't have busted out without a reason. He's got targets in mind. My guess it's you, me... anyone who crossed him.'

Kirsten swallowed hard. She had written articles about Marco's crimes, exposing his brutality to the world. If he was out for revenge, she'd be on his list. 'Thanks, Jimmy. Keep your ears open. Let me know if you hear anything else,' she said, sliding out of the booth.

Her pulse pounded in her ears. The air in the diner felt heavier, like even the walls knew too much. Jimmy had gone straight—he drove a delivery truck now, kept his head down. But the fear in his eyes told her everything she needed to know.

This was a game of life and death—one that it was far too late to leave.

By the time Kirsten made it back home, the gravity of the situation was crushing her. Marco was on the loose. And this new guy, Eddie, was a wild card.

Her phone buzzed. It was Craig.

'How's Steelvale?' she asked, anxiety creeping into her voice.

'Worse than we thought,' Craig replied tensely. 'This was planned and brilliantly co-ordinated. They had help, and they left a message.'

Kirsten gripped her phone tighter. 'What kind of message?'

Craig sighed. 'The kind that says they're not done. This is just the beginning, Kirsten. They're coming for more.'

Kirsten's breath hitched. 'We need to stop them, Craig. Before they strike again.'

'We will. But first, we must figure out where they're headed next.'

Her phone vibrated with a text. She checked it, then slung her bag over her shoulder and grabbed her keys, wedging her phone between her ear and her shoulder.

'I'm heading out, Craig,' she said, unlocking her convertible. 'I've got a source who might have something big. I'll fill you in later.'

'Kirsten, wait—' Craig started, but she had already hung up.

* * *

The underground parking garage was dimly lit, the only sound the faint hum of city life beyond the exit ramp. As Kirsten reached her car, she barely had time to process the movement in her peripheral vision before strong hands grabbed her from behind.

'Evening, princess,' a cold voice sneered in her ear.

Kirsten fought like hell, elbows flying, legs kicking, but it was two against one. Marco and Eddie forced her against the car, their laughter slicing through the air like blades.

'You are one stubborn bitch, I'll give you that,' Eddie jeered, tightening his grip.

Marco leaned in close, his breath hot against her skin. 'You really thought you could drag my name through the mud and just walk away?' His voice was a venomous whisper. 'All those bullshit articles, all those lies—painting me like some monster. Well, sweetheart, it's time you see the real me.'

'You *are* a monster,' Kirsten spat, twisting against them.

Marco gripped her jaw, forcing her to look at him. 'No, no, no. See, you chose to believe that garbage. You hardly even knew me. You just wrote whatever you wanted, and people lapped it up.' His mouth curled. 'But now... now, you get the real story.'

Eddie chuckled darkly. 'And let's just say it's got a very unhappy ending for you.'

Kirsten bucked against them, thrashing wildly. 'Screw you both!'

Marco's patience snapped. He shoved her hard against the car, yanking a blindfold over her eyes while Eddie wrestled her hands behind her back, binding them tight.

'She's a fighter,' Eddie mused. 'Gotta say, I love a little resistance.'

'Doesn't matter,' Marco said. 'She's coming with us. Far away from Craig, far away from Champaign. No one's gonna find her.'

Eddie gave a crooked smile, full of himself. 'And by the time they do, well... she won't be in any condition to write another hit piece.'

Kirsten fought back a fresh wave of panic as she felt the boot pop open. This was it. They were going to throw her in, disappear with her into the night, and no one would ever—

Then—

A deafening screech tore through the garage. Tyres screamed against concrete as a black Hummer flew down the ramp, its headlights flaring like twin white-hot eyes.

'Shit!' Eddie hissed.

Marco cursed under his breath, grabbing Kirsten by the arm, ready to drag her with them—

But the Hummer wasn't stopping.

In a split second, Marco and Eddie made their decision. They shoved Kirsten to the ground and bolted, sprinting toward a van idling just meters away. The doors slammed shut behind them, and with a roar of the engine, they sped off into the night.

Three plain-clothed detectives leaped out from the Hummer, guns drawn, scanning the lot for any more threats.

'Kirsten!' one of them called, rushing to her side.

She gasped, coughing as she ripped the blindfold off. Pain radiated through her body from the struggle. She was visibly shaken, but alive.

'Get her in the car!' another detective ordered. 'We're taking her straight to the station.'

Kirsten barely processed the words as they lifted her to her feet. The adrenaline was wearing off, and the full weight of what had almost happened crashed over her like a tidal wave.

* * *

Back at the station, Craig stormed into the room, his face tight with barely restrained fury. His hands clenched into fists when he saw

Kirsten—dishevelled, bruised, but safe.

'They were close,' one of the detectives said grimly. 'One more minute, and she would've been gone. Lucky you had a bad feeling and sent us after her.'

The tendons in Craig's neck flared. 'These bastards need to be stopped. Now.' He exhaled sharply, running a hand through his hair. 'And it's not just Kirsten. The list of targets is growing. We're running out of time.'

Kirsten swallowed hard. 'What... what do we do?'

Craig turned to the officers. His tone was unwavering. 'She goes into a safe house. Tonight. Round-the-clock supervision. No one in, no one out. We lock this down before they get another chance at her.'

No one argued.

As the team mobilized, Craig looked at Kirsten, his expression softer now, but no less determined.

'We're gonna get them, Kirst. I promise you.'

* * *

Even as he spoke, miles away in the darkness of the speeding van, Marco sat seething, fists clenched so tight his knuckles went white.

'Fuck, that was close,' he snarled, his voice low and simmering with rage. 'We needed just thirty more fucking seconds.'

Eddie shook his head, fingers wringing the steering wheel. 'We had her, man. Right there. In our hands.'

Marco's breathing was heavy, erratic. He pressed a hand to his temple, inhaled deeply, then exhaled through his nose. Slowly, his lips curled into a sinister smirk.

'Doesn't matter.' He sounded eerily calm now. 'We're not done yet.'

He turned to Eddie, eyes gleaming with a terrifying promise.

'If we can't take her tonight, we'll take someone else.'

The van tore through the night, the city lights blurring behind them.

And somewhere, in the safety of a police-protected house, Kirsten had no idea that Marco wasn't done with her yet.

Not even close.

CHAPTER 21
GHOST HUNTING

The safe house reeked of stale coffee and stress. Papers were scattered across the cluttered desk where Craig sat, poring over a mountain of intel. The dim yellow glow of the desk lamp cast sharp shadows on his face, emphasizing the deep furrow in his brow. Wind howled against the blacked-out windows, rattling the fragile calm inside. Detectives moved briskly around the room, their hushed voices blending with the constant buzz of radio chatter. Every single one of them knew what was at stake.

Craig slammed a file onto the table. 'Listen up, everyone!' His voice cut through the tension like a blade. The room fell still, all eyes on him. 'We've just received a crucial lead from one of Marco's associates. Turns out, they weren't just running for freedom. They have a damn list. A hit list.'

The atmosphere in the room shifted. A murmur rippled through the team as they exchanged uneasy glances. Kirsten, sitting stiffly on the worn-out leather couch, lifted her gaze from the case notes. Her expression was a mix of sceptical and intrigued. 'And this code?' she asked, tapping the sheet in front of her. 'The message found in Steelvale, what does it reveal?'

Craig pulled out a printed document, his fingers twitching with barely contained anticipation. 'It confirms what we suspected— someone on the outside helped them escape. A facilitator. Goes by 'A.' This person has been feeding Marco and Eddie intel and resources, making them even more dangerous.'

Kirsten's eyes darkened with sudden realization. 'Oh my God. The Architect… the head honcho and mastermind of Noctis.' The name dripped from her lips like venom. 'That weasel. That blithering snake. I knew he had their whereabouts. The bastard was stringing me along the whole damn time. Shit!' She exhaled sharply, covering her mouth as if to physically stop the flood of expletives. 'Oops, pardon my French.'

A charged silence filled the room. Craig exchanged a glance with Kirsten, the weight of the revelation pressing on them all. Marco wasn't just a fugitive; he was a predator backed by a network of shadows, supporting his ruthless ambition. This escape had purpose.

'What about Eddie?' Kirsten's voice was steady now, controlled, but the fire in her eyes was unmistakable. 'Where does he fit in all this?'

Craig leaned against the desk, mouth tight. 'Eddie is obsessed with Marco. It's beyond loyalty—it's fanaticism. Prison reports suggest he sees Marco as some kind of messiah. He doesn't have a personal vendetta, but he'd burn the world down for Marco.'

Kirsten exhaled, shaking her head. 'Great. A deranged cult of two with a hit list. Just what we need… and I saw first-hand how in sync they are. Together, they're deadly.'

'Exactly,' Craig said, straightening. 'We can't afford to waste time. I want teams on the ground now. Sweep the city for any trace of them, and send me updates every hour. We'll coordinate through central command and double security on all high-risk targets.'

A sharp knock at the door broke the moment. Officer Wesley Gwelbryn, Craig's reliable subordinate at Homicide, rushed in, breathless, holding up his tablet. 'Sir, we've intercepted new comms—Marco and Eddie are already making moves. They were spotted near the industrial district. There's chatter about a possible target.'

Craig grabbed the tablet and scanned the screen. 'They're moving faster than we thought. We can't wait for them to strike first.'

Kirsten shot up from the couch. 'To hell with the safe house, Craig. I'm coming with you.'

Craig hesitated. 'Kirsten—'

'No.' She stepped closer, her voice ironclad. 'I'm not being sidelined and stuck in here for God knows how long. You can either accept it or waste time arguing.'

Craig sighed, running a hand through his hair. He knew better than to fight her on this. 'Fine. But stay close. And if we find them—'

'We stop them,' Kirsten finished for him, grabbing her coat.

As they gathered their gear and prepared to move out, a pulse of adrenaline coursed through Craig's veins. The chase was on, and this time, he wouldn't let them slip through his fingers.

Across the city, in the depths of an abandoned warehouse, Marco and Eddie huddled over a blueprint, their hushed voices filled with calculated malice. The game had begun. They didn't know Craig was closing in. But soon, they would.

The hunt was in full swing, and justice was gaining ground. It was only a matter of time before their worlds collided once more.

*   *   *

Alessandro's wife Isabella stood on the terrace of their hillside villa in Sanremo, the scent of lemon blossoms drifting through the warm Italian air. Nearby, Alessandro was lost in thought, staring out at the glittering expanse of the Mediterranean, its waves reflecting the dying embers of the sunset. The sky was painted in gold and crimson, a breathtaking contrast to the storm brewing inside him. It had been nearly three years since he and Isabella left Champaign behind—a city steeped in memories too painful to bear after Gabriella's death. The move to Italy had been Alessandro's quiet escape, a desperate bid to outrun grief that clung to every street corner, every familiar face. Ever loyal, Isabella followed without hesitation, hoping the old stone walls and olive groves might soften what time could not heal.

But there was no telling what he was thinking. The news of Marco Carrera's escape had filled him with a deep, bone-chilling rage. It wasn't just justice that Alessandro sought. He wanted vengeance.

His fingers tightened around the iron railing as his mind replayed the images that refused to fade—crime-scene photos of the brutal home invasion, the desecration of his parents' sanctuary. The look of sheer terror on his mother's face was etched into his mind like a scar, vivid and raw.

Through the crackling video on WhatsApp, Francesca's voice had trembled as she recounted the events, each word a painful depiction of the violence bestowed on their home. Tears had streamed down her face as she spoke, her eyes haunted by the recollection. Alessandro had seen the strain in her features, the desperate need to stay strong for him, but the fear was impossible to hide. And in the background, his father had sat motionless, staring blankly at the floor, the weight of the break in suffocating him. Pepe's silence had spoken volumes; Alessandro's father, always the rock, the one who held the family together, was now a shell of the man he had been. This hadn't just been a break-in—it was an invasion of their very souls.

'Alessandro...' Francesca's voice cracked; her words shook with fear. Her English was broken, her meaning clear only through the raw panic in her eyes.

'*Loro*... they come in the night. Break the door. *Tutto distrutto*—everything... gone. *Rovistano*, make mess, take things.' She pressed a trembling hand to her chest. 'We come back... some days later. After.' Her voice dropped to a whisper. 'If... if we no change plan...' She shook her head hard. '*Madonna santa*, I—I no want think... no.'

Her voice had faltered, choking on her horror. Alessandro's fists had clenched as blood rushed to his head. He'd wanted to reach through the screen, take her in his arms, but the distance between them felt impossibly wide.

'I... I'm sorry, my son.'

Pepe's voice was barely a whisper, each word shaped like a confession. His English was slow, uncertain. 'I... I not there. Could not stop them.' He looked down, shame heavy in his eyes. '*Mi dispiace tanto.*'

The words had struck Alessandro like a fist to the chest. 'Well, thank God you weren't. Otherwise, we wouldn't be having this conversation now.'

Marco. It had to be Marco. The bastard had destroyed his family, shattered their peace, and now—he was free.

Alessandro's vision had blurred with rage.

'I swear, I'll make him pay for this,' he'd whispered to the screen, his voice low but filled with a deadly promise. His mother's tear-streaked face had flickered before him one last time, her eyes bright with fear for him, for their family.

And in that moment, Alessandro had known that he couldn't let this go. He would bring Marco down. Or he would burn everything to the ground trying.

Now, he exhaled sharply, pushing himself away from the balcony. Marco's name burned in his mind, a constant reminder that the nightmare wasn't over. Not by a long shot. He wouldn't waste another second in grief; he had spent too long mourning the death of his beloved sister Gabriella, and with this recent catastrophe, he could no longer stand on the sidelines while men like Marco thrived.

He strode back inside, his resolve hardening with every step. Gripping his keys, he kissed Isabella goodbye and headed for the place that had become his second home—the dojo.

* * *

Giovanni, a burly man with years of experience in various secret services, watched as Alessandro's fists collided with the heavy bag, each strike landing with calculated precision. The older man crossed his arms. His expression was a locked door as Alessandro pivoted, dodging an invisible opponent before delivering a brutal roundhouse kick.

'You've come a long way,' Giovanni finally said, stepping forward. 'But brute force won't be enough. Carrera's not just some street thug—he's smart. Dangerous. He plans his moves, and so should you.'

Alessandro wiped sweat from his brow, his eyes fierce with determination. 'Then let's take this to the next level. I don't just want to fight, Giovanni. I need to win.'

Giovanni studied him for a moment, then nodded. 'Alright. No more basic drills. We focus on strategy. Anticipation. You need to be faster than Marco, smarter than Marco. And, most importantly, unpredictable.'

Alessandro's jaw clenched. 'I've been unpredictable my whole life.'

Giovanni smiled like a wolf scenting blood. Then let's turn that into a weapon.'

* * *

The next few weeks pushed Alessandro beyond his limits. Giovanni put him through relentless drills—blindfolded sparring, advanced disarming techniques, psychological warfare tactics. Alessandro learned to read body language and anticipate attacks before they happened. At night, he pored over Marco's case files, memorizing his patterns, his known associates, his every move. Alessandro reached out to old contacts, tracking each strand in the web of Marco's operations. He wasn't just preparing for a fight—he was preparing for war.

And then the call came.

Alessandro's phone buzzed on the counter. He picked it up without thinking, pressing it to his ear.

'Alessandro.' The deep voice on the other end was instantly recognizable. Riaan, the police chief from Champaign.

Alessandro straightened. 'Chief.'

'I've been hearing things about your training,' Riaan said. 'We could use someone like you on the team.'

Alessandro's grip tightened around the phone. 'The team chasing Marco.'

'Exactly. The entire department is on edge. He's more dangerous than ever, and we can't afford to let him slip through our fingers again.' A pause. 'You understand why I'm calling, don't you?'

'Because I have more at stake than anyone.'

'Because you have *everything* at stake,' Riaan corrected. 'Marco took your sister. He's targeted your family. And now? Now, we know he's not done.'

Alessandro's breath came sharp. 'What are you saying?'

'We intercepted chatter,' Riaan said. 'He's expanding his hit list. And, Alessandro... your name's on it.'

A chill ran down Alessandro's spine, but he refused to let fear take root. Instead, a dangerous smirk curled at his lips.

'Then it's simple,' he said coldly. 'We strike first. I want his blood.'

Riaan chuckled darkly. 'That's what I was hoping you'd say.'

'I want in,' Alessandro said firmly. 'Not as an outsider. Not as a consultant. I want full access. Every plan, every move. I need to be part of this hunt.'

'You'll be working directly with Lieutenant Ryan and the rest of the team,' Riaan confirmed. 'We're strategizing a foolproof plan. You ready for this?'

Alessandro's eyes burned with determination.

'I was born ready.'

* * *

As Alessandro strode into Champaign PD, fresh off a full day of flights, the weight of what lay ahead pressed heavily on his chest. The atmosphere in the precinct was taut with tension. Officers hustled through the corridors, exchanging leads, discussing strategies, each of them aware that they were hunting a phantom who could strike at any moment.

Alessandro marched into the conference room, his eyes scanning the interior with practiced focus. Whiteboards covered in notes and red pins marking key locations told him everything he needed to know. Craig stood at the head of the long table, flanked by Kirsten and a handful of detectives, all of them waiting.

'Glad you could join us, Alessandro,' Craig said, his handshake firm. 'We're all aware of your personal stake in this. We need every bit of information you have on Marco.'

Alessandro met Craig's gaze, jaw set, the weight of his own vengeance now tied to this man's mission. They both had something to settle.

'Let's start with what you've gathered,' Alessandro said, his voice cutting through the tension as he took a seat at the table. 'I want to know their next move.'

Kirsten, her sharp eyes scanning the case files, spoke up. 'Marco has a network. He's not acting alone. He's part of Noctis.'

Alessandro leaned forward, his posture focused. His mind immediately clicked into the investigative mode that had taken over his life for years. 'I can help with that. In Italy, I gathered intel on Marco's operations. Yes, Kirsten, you're quite correct: he is involved with Noctis. Word has it he's The Architect's golden boy. He thrives on chaos, but it's a specific kind of chaos. He always returns to places that have meaning to him—personal, sentimental locations that make him feel untouchable.'

Craig's eyes widened slightly. Alessandro's insight was impressive. 'That's exactly what we need. We can use your knowledge of his behaviour to set a trap.'

Alessandro nodded, his thoughts already whirring. He could picture Marco's movements—how he would return to the shadows of his past, always circling back to where his violence had once taken root. Alessandro knew his patterns, the little details that might slip by everyone else.

'We need to look for places that hold meaning for him—old haunts, areas where he committed his first crimes,' Alessandro continued, his voice calm but carrying an undeniable intensity. 'We'll find him by tracking his history, his need to exert control over places he once conquered.'

The team absorbed this, their collective focus sharp as they pored over maps, cross-referencing old locations, crime scenes, and intelligence reports. The hours ticked by, but Alessandro's concentration never wavered. His mind was a machine, processing, calculating, and eliminating possibilities. His training had transformed him from a victim into something else entirely—a hunter.

'Do you think we're one step ahead of them?' Kirsten asked, her tone edged with uncertainty.

Alessandro's eyes met hers. 'We have to be.' His voice hardened. 'Marco is cunning, but he's also predictable in his brutality. He follows patterns. He craves the chaos, the spectacle of his power. If we can anticipate his moves, we can set a trap he won't see coming.'

The room fell into a heavy silence as the weight of his words settled on them. Craig, who had been watching Alessandro closely, nodded slowly. 'Then let's get to work. We've got a dangerous game to play and must be ready for anything.'

The shift in Alessandro was palpable. Every detail, every decision now mattered in ways he once couldn't have imagined. He had been trained, sharpened by months of strategy and grit. Marco wouldn't slip away again.

And for Craig, the tension was different. He had dealt with Marco's mind games before. But this time, with Alessandro on board, Craig's confidence was unshakable. He knew how to get under Marco's skin and outwit him. Marco had been playing a game for too long, but now the tables had turned.

'We're not the only players in this,' Craig said, his voice low, his eyes fierce. 'And Marco's going to learn that the hard way.'

Alessandro nodded, his face hard as granite. He could feel the old fears being buried, replaced by something far more dangerous: a burning need to take Marco down.

The plan had been set in motion. They were ready.

The hunt had begun.

CHAPTER 22
THIS TIME, IT'S PERSONAL

Champaign buzzed with the largest manhunt in Illinois history. The fervour that once gripped the city when Gabriella went missing seemed like child's play compared to what was unfolding now. Marco and Eddie, the most wanted men in the state, had slipped into the shadows, hiding near Boneyard Creek—a narrow, winding stream that snaked through the city—concealed beneath the bridge at White Street. The south end of the Boneyard Basin, with its small waterfall veiled by prairie landscaping, right in the middle of the university district, was the perfect refuge. Surrounded by students glued to their phones, oblivious to the chaos around them, Marco and Eddie felt untouchable.

Marco's eyes narrowed on the dark horizon. He exhaled slowly, a thin stream of smoke curling into the night air like a promise.

'She's the key,' he muttered, flicking the packaging from his gum to the ground. 'You wanna break a man like Craig Ryan? You don't go after him—you go after the thing he lives for.'

Eddie grinned, eyes glittering. 'Daddy's girl. Chelsea.' He spat the name. 'You sure about this?'

'We're not gonna just scare her, Eddie,' Marco said, cold and unblinking. 'We're gonna hurt her. Bad. He needs to feel it. That kind of pain... it sticks.'

Eddie whistled softly. 'You ever seen a cop unravel, Marco?

'Cause after this, we'll get front row seats.'

Marco's smile twisted. 'He should've kept his nose out of our business. Instead, he threw us to the wolves. Now we show him what consequences look like.'

They shared a silent nod, like soldiers before battle. Their target was set. Their message would be clear.

Chelsea Ryan would suffer—and her father would drown in the aftermath.

* * *

Chelsea Ryan had always carried a quiet grace that turned heads and a fierce intellect that earned respect. With flowing auburn hair that shimmered in the light and eyes the colour of a storm-tossed sea, she was striking in a way that was both elegant and disarming. Her natural beauty was matched only by her brilliance—she held a master's degree in education and had recently been shortlisted for a leadership position at a prestigious private school. But her heart—warm, loyal, and grounded—earned the love of all who knew her.

To her father, Lieutenant Craig Ryan, she was everything. Their bond was unbreakable, fortified by mutual admiration and unwavering devotion over the years. Since the brutal murders of Chelsea's closest friends in Champaign, Craig's protectiveness had intensified. All those years ago, when Marco smirked as he was being led to the holding cells, he made a crude remark about Chelsea's beauty—and Craig's blood ran cold. There were lines no man crossed, and that one had seared itself into Craig's memory like a brand. If Marco ever touched her, Craig knew he would do whatever it took to destroy him.

But Marco was already thinking ahead. It hadn't taken long for him and Eddie to track Chelsea down. A few social media breadcrumbs, a property records search, and one careless tagged photo—and they were standing outside her townhouse in the early morning hours. The silence was complete, the street deserted, the windows dark. They bypassed the alarm with calculated ease and broke in like they'd done it a hundred times before.

Inside, the tidy, half-sunlit charm of Chelsea's home was a stark contrast to the menace creeping through its halls. They rifled through her belongings, leaving deliberate signs of intrusion. Glass crunched beneath their boots as they ransacked the place with deliberate violence—drawers upturned, her books shredded, family photos defaced. The taunting was personal. A photo of Chelsea and Craig was slashed across the middle, Marco's boot print smeared across Craig's smiling face.

Chelsea had barely woken before they were on her.

She scrambled backwards, breath hitching, trying to scream— but Marco was already there, grabbing her by the throat, shoving her hard against the bed. His breath was hot against her ear.

'You should've told Daddy to stay out of our business,' he sneered, his voice low and venomous. 'But now? Now, he gets to suffer twice. First, through you... then himself.'

They attacked her with brutal, animalistic rage—blows landing without mercy, words slicing deeper than fists, brutally assaulting her. When they finally left her, she was barely conscious, curled on the cold tiles, bruised, bloodied, broken.

It took her nearly ten minutes to crawl to the bathroom. She stood under scalding water for over an hour, her skin raw and reddened, but the feeling of them still clung to her. Her hands trembled uncontrollably, her sobs muffled by the roar of the shower, but somewhere in the fog of pain, she remembered something—something important.

They'd said it. Carelessly, arrogantly.

Boneyard Creek.

She stumbled into her bedroom, half-dressed and dripping wet, and grabbed her phone with trembling fingers. Her vision swam, her thumb barely landing on the right contact.

Her breath caught in her throat as it rang once.

Twice.

'Come on,' she whispered, voice trembling, 'pick up, pick *up*—'

'Hey—' Craig's voice, calm and warm.

But her words came out in gasps, a strangled, breathless horror. 'Daddy—they... they were here. They came—Marco and Eddie—they—they hurt me, they—'

Craig's heart stopped. 'What? Chelsea, slow down. What happened? Are you hurt?'

'I—I couldn't stop them—I'm sorry—I—'

His voice shifted in an instant, ragged, sharp with panic. 'They *what?*'

She broke into sobs.

Craig went utterly silent, his knuckles white against his phone. His daughter's shattered voice was a dagger to his gut. His pulse roared in his ears. His stomach lurched.

And then—an explosion.

'I'm going to kill them.' He was trembling with fury. 'I swear to God, Chelsea. I swear to every breath I've got left—I will find them. And I will end this.'

She barely heard him through the ringing in her ears.

'They said—they're going back. To Boneyard Creek...'

Craig didn't say another word.

He was already moving.

Already loading his weapon.

Already seeing red.

Every fibre of his body screamed for blood.

CHAPTER 23
BREAKING POINT

Kirsten was already halfway down the steps of the safe house when Craig stormed out the front door, gun holstered, badge clipped, keys clenched so tightly his knuckles had gone white, heedless of the pouring rain.

'Craig!' she called, her voice cracking. 'Craig, wait!'

He didn't stop.

She caught up to him at the car and grabbed his arm. 'Don't shut me out,' she said, breathless. 'Please—don't you dare shut me out now.'

Craig froze; his jaw flexed once, then again. He couldn't look at her.

'I'm going with you,' she said, more firmly this time.

'You're not,' he growled.

'She's my goddaughter, Craig! I held her in my arms the day she was born. I love her. Don't ask me to sit here while she's out there—alone, broken—don't ask me to do that!'

He turned to her, eyes hollow with rage and pain. 'You don't want to see what I'm going to do when I find them.'

'I don't care,' she whispered. 'I'm coming. You need me. And she needs both of us.'

For a long moment, the only sound was the hiss of water on the tarmac. Then, wordlessly, he nodded.

The road blurred beneath them, headlights slicing through the rain. Craig's grip on the wheel was iron. His voice, when he finally spoke, was low and cold.

'He touched her,' he said. 'That son of a bitch laid hands on my baby girl.'

Kirsten stared straight ahead, eyes rimmed red. 'I know.'

Craig's knuckles whitened again. 'I don't want an arrest. I don't want a trial. I want Marco to feel everything he made her feel—fear, helplessness, pain. And I want him to beg for it to end.'

Kirsten didn't interrupt. She knew this wasn't a threat. It was a promise.

'I'm not a cop right now,' he added. 'I'm a father. And no jury in the world would convict me for what I'm about to do.'

Across town, the command centre was lit up like a war zone. Alessandro stood in front of the tracking board, voice clipped and urgent.

'We almost had them,' he snapped. 'Traffic cam caught them heading west out of Logan. Then they disappeared. But now—after this?'

Police Chief Riaan turned to the team, fire in his eyes. 'We'll make those bastards pay.'

A murmur of agreement rolled through the room.

Riaan pointed to the map. 'Going by our timeline, they should be back at Boneyard Creek. We sweep it *now*. Drones, dogs, boots—everything. I want them found, and I want them cornered. We don't let them disappear again.' He glanced at Alessandro. 'Craig's already en route to Chelsea. Assign backup. Discreet, but ready to move. He's not thinking straight. And I don't blame him.'

The team snapped into motion. Radios crackled. Files shuffled. Gear bags zipped.

As they poured out of the precinct in coordinated formation, boots hitting the pavement like war drums, the storm had officially broken.

This wasn't a manhunt anymore.

It was a reckoning.

It was about ending the nightmare—for Chelsea, for Craig, for everyone Marco and Eddie had terrorized.

Once and for all.

Back at Boneyard Creek, completely breathless, hearts thumping, Marco and Eddie tried to regroup. The serenity of their refuge under the bridge gave them a moment of clarity, but the untouchable feeling they once revelled in had worn thin. The heat was on, and Marco could feel the noose tightening.

'Maybe we should've waited before shaking up Chelsea,' Eddie muttered, fidgeting against the stone wall.

'They don't know where we are,' Marco said, more to convince himself than Eddie. 'We've played this game before. They're chasing shadows.'

But even Marco could hear the doubt creeping into his own voice.

A distant sound broke the uneasy silence. Footsteps—lots of them, coming toward the bridge. Marco and Eddie froze, instincts kicking in.

'They've found us,' Eddie muttered, pulling his jacket tighter.

Marco's mind raced. 'Plan B. Now.'

They moved like shadows, slipping through the late-afternoon downpour and vanishing before the officers could spot them, sprinting down the streets, adrenaline coursing through their veins. Every second felt like a ticking bomb. Marco's heart pounded like artillery fire as they leaped over hedges and barrelled through alleys, knocking over trash cans in their desperate bid to reach the car their contact Giles had stashed three blocks away. The urgency in their steps was palpable; they couldn't afford a single mistake.

'Faster!' Marco hissed at Eddie, who was just a second behind, clutching his side as they approached the corner.

'There!' Eddie pointed. They skidded to a stop in front of an old, beat-up sedan parked under a flickering lamppost.

Marco quickly crouched by the rear wheel, finding the keys where Giles said they'd be. 'Got 'em!' he shouted as he tossed them into the air, catching them mid-flip before jumping into the driver's seat. Eddie slid in next to him, panting, eyes darting nervously in every direction.

'Go, go, go!' Eddie urged, adrenaline surging through his veins.

Marco jammed the key into the ignition, his hands trembling as the seconds ticked away. For a heart-stopping moment, nothing happened.

Then the engine roared with a deafening growl.

'Move it!' Eddie yelled, his voice barely audible over the rumble of the engine.

Marco slammed the accelerator to the floor, the tyres screeching on the wet asphalt as they peeled out in a cloud of smoke and burning rubber. The car shot forward like a bullet, weaving through narrow streets, barely missing parked cars and dumpsters, their surroundings a blur of shadows and neon lights. Every nerve was on edge, but so far, no sirens were chasing them. The further they got from Boneyard Creek, the quieter the city became.

They weren't just running now—they were flying!

CHAPTER 24
INTO THE GREY

Eddie looked over at Marco, smirking. 'I can't believe we got away. That was some next-level shit back there.'

'Don't get too comfortable yet,' Marco replied, eyes locked on the road ahead. 'We're not out of the woods until we're far away from this fucking city.'

They weaved through traffic, blending in with the early evening commuters. For once, Marco's white-knuckled driving didn't make them stand out. They sped through intersections and skirted past red lights, their escape merging seamlessly with the city's quiet chaos.

It wasn't until they reached the outskirts of town that they allowed themselves a breath of relief. The skyline of Champaign faded in the rearview mirror, and the tension in the car finally eased.

Marco glanced at Eddie. 'We'll split the driving. Four hours each. Sound good?'

Eddie snorted, leaning back in his seat. 'Hell yeah, but I'll take the second shift. You drive like a grandma, so I might as well catch some sleep while you putter along.' He cracked a grin and closed his eyes.

'Whatever, you dick,' Marco muttered, shaking his head but unable to hide his snicker.

Eight hours later, as the night sky gradually yielded to dawn, they arrived in Sault Ste. Marie, a small, quiet Michigan town right on the Canadian border. It appeared to be the ideal cover. Eddie followed Giles's instructions meticulously, driving directly to the safe house—an old and secluded shack, its faded exterior merging with the surrounding trees.

As they pulled up, a figure stepped out from the shadows of the porch. Todd, a Noctis fixer, was waiting for them, arms crossed, a cigarette dangling from his lips.

'You two certainly don't mess around,' Todd said, extending a hand. Marco and Eddie each shook it, grateful for the warm welcome. 'You've done well to get here. Lie low tonight, and at first light, we'll cross the bridge.'

Marco furrowed his brow. 'The bridge?'

'Yeah, my pickup is parked out back. You'll ride under the tarp. I know everyone at the border crossing, so you two just need to stay out of sight. Once we're on the Canadian side of Sault Ste. Marie, my associate in Ontario will meet you there. You'll be on your way to Thunder Bay by noon.' Todd's voice lowered as he stubbed out his cigarette. 'And listen—Leo, my associate, is getting you Canadian passports. You'll be ready to fly out to Reykjavik in two days. From there, you'll head to London.'

Eddie nodded eagerly. 'Two days and we're out of here, huh? Sounds like a dream.'

Todd's expression changed. 'One last thing. Leo's doing you a favour, but it ain't free. You settle his bill before you board that flight. No dough, no freedom. You understand?'

Marco exchanged a look with Eddie. 'We get it.'

'Good,' Todd said, no smile this time. 'Get some rest. We leave at dawn.'

* * *

Morning arrived faster than expected. By 5:00 a.m., they were crammed into the back of Todd's pickup, concealed under a tarp like cargo. The air was chilly, and Marco's breath escaped in visible puffs as he shifted uncomfortably next to Eddie.

'Are you good?' Marco whispered.

Eddie nodded, though his body was tense. 'Let's just get this over with.'

They could hear the rumble of the truck's engine and feel every bump in the road as they approached the bridge. Marco's heart pounded in his chest. Any slip-up, any misstep, and they were finished.

The truck slowed as it approached the crossing.

'Here we go,' Marco muttered.

From beneath the tarp, they heard muffled voices. Todd spoke to the border guard, calm and collected as always. It felt like an eternity passed before they heard the truck start rolling again. Marco dared to peek out from under the tarp and saw the bridge fading into oblivion.

'We're in Canada,' Marco whispered, his voice filled with disbelief.

Eddie cracked a grin. 'Hell yeah, man. We did it.'

* * *

The cabin wasn't much to look at—just a derelict fishing lodge swallowed by pine trees, somewhere in the wilderness outside Thunder Bay—but it was warm, remote, and stocked with enough peanut butter and instant noodles to feed a small cult. Todd had done his part.

Marco stepped inside, dropped his duffel, and sniffed. 'Smells like a taxidermist's armpit in here.'

Eddie shut the door behind him and peered at the dusty wood-panelled walls. 'You'd think, for a 'safe house,' there'd be less mould and more safety.'

Just then, the front door banged open. In swept a whirlwind of auburn curls, oversized sunglasses, and faux fur that looked like it had seen Vegas and never emotionally recovered.

'Gentlemen,' said the woman in a lilting French-Canadian accent, peeling off her gloves with dramatic flair. 'You look like two abandoned gym bags. Let's fix that.'

Marco blinked. 'You're... Kimmi?'

'You were expecting James Bond? Please, sit down. Don't talk. I need full concentration.'

She dragged a battered suitcase across the floor, popped it open, and revealed enough beauty tools to outfit a drag show. Razors, wigs, colour contacts, tweezers, contour palettes, brow stencils, scissors, temporary tattoos, and even a prosthetic nose or two.

'You're not transforming us,' Eddie said, eyeing a glue stick with suspicion. 'You're rebuilding us.'

'Oui,' Kimmi said brightly, already spritzing Marco's face with rosewater. 'And you'll thank me when you're both hotter, safer, and complete strangers to the Steelvale mugshots.'

CHAPTER 25
THREADS OF THE NET

Back in Champaign, the dismay was palpable as news of Marco and Eddie's escape flashed across every screen in the precinct. Phones buzzed, voices overlapped, and every officer on duty scrambled to understand how this could happen again.

Riaan stood by the window, watching the chaos unfold, his face tight with frustration. 'These two make Houdini look like a left-hand throw, slipping through our fingers three times,' he muttered, shaking his head. 'It's like they're coated in Teflon. We'll be a laughingstock if we don't get these fuckers. I'm stunned.'

'You're not the only one, Chief,' Craig said, leaning against the door frame, his expression hard.

Riaan stepped closer to the board. A hush enveloped the room as he addressed it, voice low but filled with the weight of command. 'Here's how it's gonna go down. We've set up roadblocks—coordinated, staggered, and quick. If there are any sightings or tips, they'll get rerouted straight to us. There are eyes on every stretch of highway between here and the border. And if the bastards go off-road, we've got dogs ready to track them.'

Craig added, 'We've also got drones. High-speed chases are too risky with civilians, but we'll track them from the sky if necessary. We won't lose them again.'

'And no messing around,' Riaan warned. 'The moment we've got a lead, we move fast. I don't care if it's the middle of the night.

We're not waiting for permission this time.'

Craig grabbed a whiteboard marker and sketched escape routes, contacts, and timelines. 'Here's what we've got so far. We're throwing everything at this. County alerts sent out—done. Checkpoints established on every major road—done. Warden Clanwell's Interpol contact is on standby, and Wesley's already working the Canadian angle. We must assume the fuckers are looking to cross into Ontario; there's no way they're staying local. Alessandro's already flown up there. Maybe he can teach us some of those Italian swear words. They sound so much more refined than when we do it. Dignified, even.' Despite his quips, his eyes held no trace of amusement.

'Yeah, no kidding,' Riaan said, pacing the room. 'Alessandro's got a temper, but he knows how to track these guys. He's already mapped out half the grid they could be in. If anyone can close in on them, it's him.'

Sitting forward, Kirsten folded her arms on the table. 'And what about the airports? They're not stupid. They'll avoid anywhere they'll have to show ID.'

'Exactly,' Craig said. 'That's why Alessandro's chasing down contacts at the border. They'll need a vehicle, something low-key. We need to hit the black market and anyone who might sell fake documents. Clanwell's got an inside man working the docks, but I'm betting those two thugs will try land routes first. I'm sending a team to every known exit—official and unofficial. We'll have agents in plain clothes. No way they're slipping out without us knowing.'

Riaan stopped pacing and turned to Craig, a glint of determination in his eyes. 'We need to cut off their supply lines. No more money, no more allies. They'll be desperate. And desperate people make mistakes.' He went to his desk, rifling through the files, pulling out the contacts known to help fugitives.

Craig nodded, his expression growing sharper, more intense. 'Once they make that mistake, we're there. We must treat this like a net. We close in tighter and tighter, suffocating them from every angle until there's nowhere left to run.'

Riaan dropped the files on his desk, fists clenching. 'And when we get them, no more Steelvale. No more cushy prisons. It's a one-way trip to Guantanamo. There's no escaping from that place; you know it, I know it, and once we have them, they'll know it too.'

The door swung open, and Wesley stormed in, waving a phone. 'Got a hit. Interpol's tracking chatter. Seems like the assholes have got a contact in Sault Ste. Marie, their window to Canada. If we can intercept them before they hit the bridge, we've got them. Alessandro's already coordinating with the Canadian Border Services, but we need to be faster—they won't wait long.'

Riaan snapped into action. 'Then we move. Craig, mobilize the teams. I want boots on the ground at Sault Ste. Marie, *now!* Wesley, get eyes on any safe houses or known contacts in the area. We need to be there when they show up.'

Craig was already on the phone, issuing orders, his voice rising above the din as the precinct exploded with activity. 'I want every available officer at that bridge! Keep it low profile, no flashy lights. We don't want them to get spooked.'

The fire inside Craig burned hotter. The hunt was back on; this time, he wouldn't just catch them but ensure they never escaped again.

'They think they're invincible,' Riaan muttered, staring at the map. 'But we'll show them how wrong they are.'

Craig nodded, his eyes steely, as he ended the call. 'This is it. No more games. We bring them in, dead or alive.'

'Alive. So we can watch them rot in Guantanamo.' Riaan grabbed his jacket, his movements deliberate and sharp, and motioned for Craig to follow. 'We're gonna need every available hand on this, and we need to move fast. Let's make *damn sure* they don't slip through again.'

CHAPTER 26
THE MASK FITS

Marco was up first. Kimmi shaved his beard, lightened his hair three shades, and cut it short on the sides with a floppy fringe up front. She gave him olive-tinted contacts, glued a faint scar onto his chin, and added faint freckles across his cheeks. Eddie lounged in a plaid recliner, eating Pringles and narrating.

'She's giving you YouTube-influencer realness, bro. You look like someone who vapes and has commitment issues.'

Marco grunted. 'Better than looking like a backup dancer for Smash Mouth.'

Kimmi turned. 'Next!'

Eddie took his seat like he was being marched to an electric chair. 'Do your worst. Just don't touch my eyebrows. They're perfect.'

Three hours later, Eddie had short jet-black hair slicked back from his forehead, a fake silver hoop in his nose, and tortoiseshell glasses with non-prescription lenses. Kimmi had given him a soul patch ('Just trust me.'), a spray tan two shades too dark ('Chic and criminal-proof!'), and a slight limp. Not real, but 'convincing for customs.'

By the end of the day, the mirror reflected two entirely new men.

Marco stared at himself. 'I look like I manage an indie bookstore and have strong opinions about herbal tea.'

Eddie raised an eyebrow at his own reflection. 'I look like I'd try to sell you crypto at a wedding.'

Kimmi clapped her hands. 'Magnifique! Now, photo time!'

They posed in front of a wrinkled white sheet taped to the wall. Marco blinked in every flash. Eddie made duck lips until Kimmi threw a hairbrush at him.

The following hours were spent lying low—no phones, no internet; just card games, bad TV, and Todd occasionally showing up to drop off 'supplies,' which included beef jerky, a taser, and a bottle of lavender bubble bath 'for stress.'

* * *

Two days later, Marco adjusted his new wire-rimmed glasses and stared up at the departures board of Thunder Bay Airport. 'Reykjavík via Toronto. Gate 7. This is really happening.'

Eddie clutched his new passport like it might sprout wings and fly away. 'I swear, if security stops me, I'm just gonna start crying and yell, 'I'm from Winnipeg!''

Marco chuckled, nerves still buzzing. 'I still can't believe Leo pulled it off.'

'Leo's a genius,' Eddie said. 'A morally ambiguous, emotionally stunted genius—but a genius.'

Kimmi strolled up to them in anything but civilian clothes, dragging a leopard-print carry-on suitcase that squeaked every few steps and chewing bright pink gum like she hadn't just orchestrated an international disappearance. She wore a skin-tight, metallic gold jumpsuit that shimmered like molten foil every time she moved, paired with a cropped faux-fur jacket in electric blue that looked like it belonged to a forgotten '80s pop star. Her heels—towering, rhinestone-encrusted stilettos—clicked dramatically on the tiles as if she were walking a runway, not slipping through the busy airport concourse. Giant gold hoop earrings bobbed with her every exaggerated chew, and of course, her signature oversized sunglasses swallowed half her face, despite her being inside a building.

'You two act like you've never seen style under pressure,' she muttered, blowing a bubble and letting it pop loudly as she caught up with her latest creations—unbothered, unapologetic, and absolutely unmistakable.

'You boys clean up very well. And Marco—remember, you're now Mathieu Rousseau, from Quebec City. You own a boutique goat cheese company.'

'Goat cheese?'

'Oui. Be confident in your cheese. Customs agents respect confidence. And you, Eddie, are Marc-Andre Leclerc, from Halifax.'

'So, what do I do?' Eddie asked.

Kimmi grinned, flicking her locks back. 'You own a pet crematorium and taxidermy studio Called 'Final Fur-well'. Right up your alley, isn't it? You can even write haiku for every animal you cremate, and you don't even have to admit that you hate cats!'

A voice came over the intercom: 'Icelandair Flight 232 to Reykjavík is now boarding.'

Eddie glanced at Marco. 'Ready to leave behind Steelvale, Champaign, and everything else that nearly got us killed?'

Marco exhaled slowly, nodding. 'Hell yes. But we'll be back.'

As they walked toward the gate, Eddie muttered, 'If they serve goat cheese on the flight, I'm telling them you made it.'

Marco grinned. 'Only if you promise to limp dramatically through customs.'

Behind, Kimmi watched them go with a small, proud smile—then turned and disappeared into the crowd.

They handed over their passports. The agent barely looked up. Stamped. Stamped.

They were through.

As they stepped onto the jet bridge, Eddie whispered, 'What's the Icelandic word for 'freedom'?'

Marco shrugged. 'No idea. But I'm pretty sure it sounds like a sigh of relief.'

CHAPTER 27
EIGHT HOURS TO BURN

Marco shoved his backpack into the overhead locker, then flopped into his seat with a dramatic groan. Eddie slid in next to him, glanced around, and whispered, 'If anyone asks, we're on a spiritual retreat to cleanse our chakras in the hot springs.'

Marco raised an eyebrow. 'I thought I was a goat cheese mogul?'

Eddie grinned. 'Multi-dimensional man. Cheese on weekdays, crystals on weekends.'

The flight attendant passed by and offered complimentary Icelandic water in small bottles that looked like they were meant for dolls. Eddie took one and muttered, 'Wow. Hydration by IKEA.'

Marco sipped his and frowned. 'This tastes like disappointment. But anyways, IKEA is Swedish, you douche.'

They settled in as the plane took off and the lights dimmed. Eddie pulled out the in-flight magazine and began flipping through. 'Okay,' he said, 'here are our options once we land: we can go to the Phallological Museum...'

'The *what*?'

Eddie held up the page. 'Yup. Museum of penises. World's largest collection. Actual quote: 'From hamster to whale."

Marco burst out laughing. 'That's... ambitious. Are we really doing that on the run?'

'Why not?' Eddie shrugged. 'No one's looking for us among

Icelandic penis enthusiasts.'

Marco wiped a tear from his eye. 'That's our next alias. 'Welcome to the Reykjavik Dick Club."

'Honestly? Could be a great cover.'

They both settled back into their seats, giggling like teenagers until Marco's stomach growled loudly.

'Mealtime,' Eddie whispered. 'Bet it's fermented shark and cloud bread.'

'Just give me something not wrapped in sadness,' Marco said.

When the meal came—a sort-of-sandwich, sort-of-mystery—they both took one bite and silently pushed their trays away.

'Now I understand why the Vikings were always so angry,' Eddie muttered.

* * *

After clearing passport control at Keflavík Airport—where Marco nailed the goat cheese backstory, and Eddie almost screwed up, but managed to pull through—they stepped out into the brisk Icelandic air, wide-eyed and slightly giddy.

'Okay,' Eddie said, rubbing his hands together, 'we've got eight hours. What do two fugitives do in the land of ice and Björk?'

'First, we blend in. Which, ironically, means acting like we don't care about anything. Zero emotion. Icelanders are cool. Stoic. Possibly immortal.'

'I can do stoic,' Eddie said. He struck a pose and said in a monotone: 'I feel nothing. I am cold and dead inside. But in a chic way.'

They found a shuttle into the city and walked around the vibrant streets of Reykjavík—full of colourful houses, puffin-themed merchandise, and locals wrapped in so many layers they looked like fashionable burritos.

At one point, Eddie dragged Marco into a tourist shop.

'You need a disguise for Heathrow,' he insisted. 'This puffin hat will save your life.'

Marco deadpanned, 'A puffin hat is not going to save my life.'

'Not with that attitude.'

Eventually, they ended up soaking in a steamy geothermal footbath in a public park, mist curling around them like a dream.

Marco leaned back, eyes closed. 'You know, if someone told me a month ago I'd be hiding from the Feds and the police while marinating my feet in volcanic water in Iceland... I'd have said, 'Yeah, sounds about right."

Eddie grinned. 'Just wait till we get to London and open our artisanal goat cheese and crypto shop.'

They sat in silence for a moment, letting the warmth seep into their bones. Then Eddie said softly, 'We made it out.'

Marco nodded. 'We're not free yet, but... yeah. We're getting there.'

Eddie nudged him. 'London's just the next chapter, man. We'll lie low, get new gigs, maybe rent a flat above a pub. You can date a brooding British librarian. I'll join a ska band.'

A smug curl played at the corner of Marco's mouth.' You'd last five minutes in a ska band.'

'Bold of you to assume I wouldn't *start* the ska band, with my incredible voice and infectious melodies.'

They both laughed. For the first time in weeks, maybe months, they weren't running. They were just... existing. Together. In Iceland. Wearing puffin hats and soaking their feet like champs.

The big screen in Champaign PD's tactical room flickered with grainy shots of a dark sedan speeding past a gas station on the outskirts of Ironwood, Michigan, timestamped three days ago.

'That's them,' Wesley confirmed, zooming in on the license plate. 'We've got partials—matches the burner vehicle on the footage three blocks away from Boneyard Creek. These guys aren't amateurs.'

Riaan stood with arms crossed, mouth tight, staring at the footage. 'How the hell are they still one step ahead? The Architect's feeding them intel.'

'Or an internal leak?' Craig asked, his tone sharp.

'Possibly,' Riaan replied. 'I want a background check of all our employees anywhere near the chase—officers, janitors, admin. Get me the financials, phone logs, everything. Scrub it clean.'

Craig nodded, already on the move, and Wesley hurried out.

A sergeant stepped in from the hallway, breathless. 'We've tapped into the Canadian Border Services feed at the Sault border. They've picked up chatter about a flight, possibly out of Thunder Bay. Could be a decoy, but it's our strongest lead yet.'

'Get it confirmed,' Riaan barked. 'I want eyes on the tarmac, immigration control, and any airstrip within a hundred-mile radius. I want those terminals locked down tighter than Fort Knox.'

Craig, multitasking with two phones, relayed orders. 'Activate the Mobile Tactical Unit. I want aerial reconnaissance drones prepped and launched within the hour. Night-vision, thermal—use the works.'

'And bring in canine units,' Riaan added. 'If they're still on foot or hiding near the border, we'll flush them out like rats.'

Just then, Wesley burst back in through the door, holding a fresh printout. 'Interpol pinged again. Passports tied to known trafficker aliases—names used in Vienna last year. 'Marc-Andre Leclerc' and 'Mathieu Rousseau.' Canadian identities confirmed as fakes. They're heading to Reykjavík.'

Riaan's fist slammed onto the desk. 'Son of a bitch. We've officially crossed the threshold into transnational criminal territory.'

Craig exhaled through gritted teeth. 'Call in the feds. Get Homeland back on the line. This just jumped three levels up.'

'The help these monsters get is endless,' Riaan muttered, pacing the room like a caged animal. 'Money, documentation, travel clearance—all fake, but it's smooth. Too smooth. Noctis's reach stretches infinitely, and that fucking bloody Architect is bankrolling this.'

Wesley added, 'Alessandro's reached out to Canadian intelligence, and CSIS is now involved. If the bastards make it to Reykjavík, we might need Icelandic cooperation, too. This is getting bigger by the minute.'

Craig clicked his pen repeatedly, adrenaline coursing through him. 'We're losing the window. Every second counts.'

Riaan's eyes swept the room—officers on comms, analysts mapping out heat signatures, maps riddled with pins and highlighted routes. 'Bring the heat,' he ordered. 'Red alert. All precincts. I want rolling checkpoints from Michigan to Ontario.

Alert the Canadian Police and freeze outbound flights from Thunder Bay. No one leaves without a face scan. We control the exits.'

'And if they slip through?' Craig asked.

'They won't.'

A long silence settled before the tactical radio crackled to life.

'Unit Bravo Six reporting from Thunder Bay. We've got unconfirmed visual on suspects leaving a cabin yesterday. Repeating—potential sighting of Marco and Eddie, moving west on Route 41 in a dark blue Chevy Cruze. Partial plate—K19. Trajectory heads to the airport.'

Craig and Riaan locked eyes.

'Let's go,' Riaan said, grabbing his tactical vest. 'Get the chopper prepped. We're not watching this from the sidelines.'

Craig snatched the whiteboard marker and underlined one phrase on the wall map: *'No Escape.'*

* * *

Craig and Riaan were moments away from boarding the chopper to Thunder Bay, their gear slung over their shoulders, minds focused on the hunt. The rotors were already beating like a countdown to war, the wind from the blades whipping across the tarmac. The mission was set, their eyes locked on Canada, on Thunder Bay, where the next lead pointed.

And then, out of nowhere, Kirsten tore across the tarmac, sprinting toward the chopper like her life depended on it, lips pressed into a hard line, eyes blazing with purpose. But it was the man beside her who stopped Craig in his tracks.

Jimmy.

Kirsten's shadowy contact—someone Craig had never met, only heard about in urgent whispers—was finally stepping out of the fog. Dressed in black, unassuming, Jimmy looked more like a mid-level banker than a man previously tied to the underbelly of the international crime web, but his presence alone made the air shift.

Kirsten spoke first, breathless. 'You need to hear the info Jimmy just gave me.'

Jimmy nodded once, solemn. 'You're not heading to Thunder Bay. Not yet. You're heading into the belly of it all. We got your man.'

Was this a lifeline in a world of shadows—or the last breadcrumb before the truth disappeared for good?

For Craig, it was enough. One name. One direction. One man who lit the fuse.

'Say that again,' he ordered. 'Now.'

Kirsten stepped forward, her voice low but brimming with fire. 'As we speak, Alessandro's bringing in Giles—the first link in the chain. The getaway car three blocks from Boneyard Creek? That was him. But it goes deeper. He mapped the entire sequence—the safehouses, the couriers, every operative in Canada. He didn't just help them vanish. He made sure no one would ever find them.'

Craig snapped his head toward her, stunned. 'Jesus. The ghost in the machine. And we've got him?'

Kirsten gave a grim nod. 'Alessandro's got him and they're headed to the station. We're about to blow this thing wide open.'

'Oh my God,' Craig said, exhaling sharply. 'Talk about the goddamn eleventh hour!' He spun on his heel. 'Chief—SUV's still on the tarmac. Let's roll.'

Riaan nodded. Craig turned to Kirsten with a rare, grateful flicker in his eyes. 'Kirst, we'll see you at the station. Tell Alessandro to stall Giles until I get there. I want the first crack.'

They lunged into motion, urgency fuelling every step.

CHAPTER 29
LOOSE ENDS AND LOCKED EYES

Sirens wailed and lights cut through the fading dusk as the SUV tore down the city streets like a bullet. Craig gripped the dash as if it might launch him into the interrogation room. Every red light was a target. Every second was a countdown.

The SUV made it to the station in record time. Screeching to a halt, it threw out adrenaline, blue strobes, and one very pissed-off detective.

Craig didn't wait for the engine to die. He was already inside. Already moving.

The real game had just begun.

* * *

The softly glowing room hummed with the low buzz of fluorescent lights. When Craig barged in, Alessandro was waiting in one shadowed corner, leaning against the wall, expression in stark contrast to his casual pose. Giles was slouched in a chair, his hands cuffed to the table. His face was pale, and a sheen of sweat glistening on his forehead, but his defiance hadn't yet cracked. He wasn't going to give anything up easily.

Craig lunged forward, his boots heavy against the concrete floor. He stopped directly in front of Giles, leaning in close enough for the man to feel the heat of his fury.

'You're going to tell me everything,' Craig growled, his voice low and cold. 'Every last detail. Or I swear to God, Giles, I will make your life a living hell until you wish you'd never been born.'

Giles swallowed hard, his attention darting to the door, the single exit that he'd never get through. 'I don't know what you're talking about.'

Craig's eyes locked onto his. 'You're not leaving here until you tell me about the car—the one you left waiting for Marco and Eddie close to Boneyard Creek.'

As Giles shook his head, a nervous chuckle escaped his lips. 'You think I'm gonna talk just because you—'

Craig slammed his fist down on the table with a deafening crash, sending a jolt of panic through Giles. He flinched but didn't speak. Craig took a slow, deliberate step back, eyes narrowed like a predator on the hunt.

'The car was just the beginning, wasn't it?' Craig's voice had dropped to a whisper, so chilling it was worse than a shout. 'You helped them escape—you started this whole fucking chain of events. You're going to tell me who else was involved. And you're going to do it now, Giles, or I swear I'll break every single bone in your body.'

Giles recoiled, visibly trembling, but his lips were still sealed. Craig leaned forward again, his breath hot on Giles's face. 'Where did they go, Giles? My patience is running out.'

The silence hung heavy, suffocating. Then, with a resigned sigh, Giles finally spoke, his voice unsteady.

'Sault Ste. Marie. They went there first, to the Michigan side. Met a guy named Todd.' He paused, his eyes darting nervously. 'After that, they... they crossed into Canada. Went north to Thunder Bay.'

Craig's stare was unmoving, unblinking. 'Who else did they meet?'

Giles started singing like a little canary.

'Leo,' he muttered. 'Leo was in Thunder Bay. He... he set them up with fake passports. They were going to London, I think.'

Craig's heart pounded in his chest. London. The international escape was beginning to make sense. He leaned in closer, demanding more. 'And from Thunder Bay? Where did they go?'

'Reykjavík,' Giles whispered, his voice barely audible. 'From there... they're headed for London.'

Mind racing, Craig stood up straight, his voice harsh now. 'You're telling me Marco and Eddie are already in London?'

Sweat was pouring down Giles's face. 'I don't know, okay? I don't know if they've made it there yet. But that's what Leo set up for them. They're gone. Gone, Lieutenant. Fake names, fake passports, fake everything. There's nothing you can do.'

Craig drove his fist into the table again, sending an empty coffee cup skittering across its surface. 'You've made sure of that, haven't you? You've covered their tracks every step of the way.'

Giles didn't say anything, his expression a mixture of fear and resignation. But Craig wasn't done. Not yet.

'And Todd—where do I find him?' Craig demanded.

'I don't know,' Giles replied quickly. 'I never met him. I don't even know where he's from. Just... just that he set them up.'

There was more to this—so much more. But Craig had what he needed for now.

'You made a huge mistake,' he said, his voice dripping with venom. 'You will regret it, Giles. I'll make sure of that.'

Giles shuddered, his eyes brimming with tears. 'Please—please, let me go. I've told you what you need to know. You've turned me into a snitch. I'm just a player... I follow orders; I don't make the rules.'

This time, Craig's voice was low, lethal—rage honed to a razor's edge. 'Don't insult me. I know you're lying about his whereabouts. I know you're sitting on information that could crack this wide open. And more importantly—I know your position in the cabal. Not speculation. Not guesswork. I *know*. You still think you're insulated, protected by layers of shadows and middlemen. You think your fingerprints won't show. But here's what you don't understand, Giles—your safety net just caught fire. And I'm the one holding the match.'

Giles looked up at him, confusion written all over his face. Craig didn't waste another second. He leaned in, eyes cold as ice, and delivered the fatal truth.

'You're Noctis's problem now, pal. You'll probably be dead within twenty-four hours—no questions asked. So don't worry about me booking you, Giles. Worry about how you're going to spend your last few hours on this earth.'

Giles's face went ashen. His breath caught, eyes wide in terror. 'No... no, no, please. I didn't—'

'You aided and abetted,' Craig said, his voice like gravel. 'You crossed the line. And now you're dead the second you step out of here.'

Giles sank back in his chair, his whole body shaking. Craig didn't spare him another glance. He turned on his heel, his steps echoing in the silence, Alessandro slipping after him like a shadow. It was already too late for Giles.

As Craig left the interrogation room, his phone buzzed in his pocket. The trail was clearer now, but his anger was far from satisfied.

Marco and Eddie were out there somewhere—and Craig was flying to London with Alessandro at his side. Not just to find them... but to end them.

CHAPTER 30
TERMINAL VELOCITY

'Yee-haw! Heathrow, here we come!' Marco whooped, flinging his arms up and startling a couple in the row ahead of him.

'Calm down, bud. We're not there yet,' Eddie muttered, grinning, as he elbowed Marco in the ribs.

Marco couldn't help it. The weight of success was intoxicating. They'd done it: escaped Steelvale, slipped through the cracks from Sault Ste. Marie to Thunder Bay, then leapt across the Atlantic with slick new identities and clean paperwork. Once they touched down in London and met Danny, one of Noctis's British operatives, they'd be ghosts.

Their flight was smooth, uneventful—until it wasn't.

They landed early, thanks to strong tailwinds, and glided through customs with an ease that made Marco even cockier. Dressed to blend in—jeans, hoodies, baseball caps pulled low—they drifted into the terminal, making their way to the agreed meet-point: WHSmith, alongside the concourse in Terminal 5.

Marco strutted ahead, fake passport tucked in his inner jacket pocket, a wicked grin on his face. 'Crime novels. Fitting, don't you think?' he muttered, leading Eddie toward the shelves stacked with violent fiction.

Eddie chuckled, chewing on a strip of gum. 'Let's just get Danny and bounce, yeah?'

But something in Marco's gut twisted. He scanned the terminal.

Too many uniforms. Too many plainclothes-looking types pretending not to look like plainclothes types.

He checked his watch. Danny was late.

'Something's wrong,' he muttered.

Eddie raised an eyebrow. 'What do you mean?'

'Shut up. Just... listen.'

That's when it hit—the rising tide of shouting, whistling, boots thudding hard against tiles. Marco's blood ran cold.

Craig Ryan stormed into view, eyes locked on his target like a laser sight. His badge was visible, his weapon drawn low but steady.

'Marco Carrera!' Craig's voice thundered through the concourse, a relentless thrum pulsing with intent. 'You're under arrest for the escape of the decade, you slippery bastard!'

Eddie bolted. Marco turned to follow, but—

Alessandro appeared out of nowhere, tackling Eddie with the force of a freight train. They crashed into a stand of travel pillows and headphones, sending merchandise flying as Alessandro twisted Eddie's arm behind his back.

'Get off me!' Eddie screamed, flailing. 'You don't know who you're messing with!'

'Oh, I know exactly who I'm messing with,' Alessandro growled, smashing Eddie's face to the floor. 'You're the jackass who ran. Big mistake.'

Marco took two steps, but Craig was already on him.

'You're done, Carrera,' Craig snarled, grabbing him by the jacket and slamming him against the crime shelf. 'No more Houdini acts. No more midnight strolls out of maximum security.'

Craig squeezed the cuffs on with brutal precision. Marco hissed, his wrists straining—until Craig yanked him closer, his voice like venom-coated steel.

'You thought you'd walk away after what you did to her?' Craig's eyes burned with raw fury. 'You and your pathetic little sidekick thought you could touch my daughter—*my daughter*—and get away with it?'

Marco froze.

'You put your filthy hands on her. You beat her. I can't even bring myself to say the rest. You left her bleeding on the goddamn floor, like trash.' Craig's voice cracked, the pain catching up with the rage. 'You don't just deserve prison—you deserve to die screaming.'

Marco swallowed. A pulse jumped at his temple as his jaw tensed.

'I've killed men for less,' Craig spat. 'I've buried people and slept like a baby. And trust me, there's nothing I want more than to put a bullet through your skull right now and dump your body in the Thames.' He shoved Marco harder into the shelf, his breath heaving. 'But you're not worth the aftermath. So, I'm going to do the next best thing.'

Craig's voice dropped to a vicious whisper. 'I'm going to put you in a hole so deep you'll forget what daylight feels like. Guantanamo. No trial. No press. No name... no rights... and no way out. I hope you scream every night. I hope you beg. Because she still hears your voice in her nightmares.'

Marco sneered, but his eyes were flickering. 'You're going to regret this,' he muttered. 'One day, you'll look over your shoulder, and—'

Craig cut him off with a cold laugh. 'The only thing I'll regret is not pulling the trigger.'

He and Alessandro frog-marched the pair out through the crowd, every step echoing like a funeral bell. Passengers gawked. Security swarmed. But they didn't stop moving.

When they reached the private FBI jet waiting on the tarmac, Craig glanced at Alessandro. 'These fuckers thought this would end with them sipping pints in a London pub. Turns out, it ends with steel bars, orange jumpsuits and hot Cuban air.'

Alessandro snorted. 'Should've packed sunscreen.'

They shoved their shackled, furious prisoners onto the jet. Eddie wouldn't stop whining. Marco sat mutely, eyes narrowed like blades, calculating... always calculating.

As the engines roared to life and the wheels left the ground, Craig glanced across the aisle, meeting Marco's icy stare.

'You don't get to win this time,' Craig hissed.

Marco leaned forward, voice deadly soft. 'We'll see about that.'

CHAPTER 31
TWO STRIKES FROM DISASTER

The flight to Guantanamo Bay felt endless. Marco and Eddie now both sat in grim silence, each lost in thought, the weight of their fate hanging over them like a death sentence. Their days of running, hiding, and scheming were a thing of the past. The word 'freedom' no longer existed in their world. They knew it, felt it in their bones, as the shackles around their wrists and ankles seemed to tighten with every passing minute.

Craig sat near the cockpit, watching the two fugitives like a hawk. Alessandro reclined beside him, head leaned back, eyes closed—but Craig knew he wasn't sleeping.

Then the cockpit door opened.

'Lieutenant Ryan,' the pilot called out, voice clipped. 'Secure call from Washington. They say it's urgent.'

Craig rose, instinct prickling. 'Put it through.'

He stepped inside the cockpit, sealing the door behind him. A soft click, then static—and finally, a voice. Calm. Clinical. Unfamiliar.

'Lieutenant Ryan. New orders. Prisoners are to be terminated mid-air.'

Craig froze. 'What the hell did you just say?'

'You heard me. Marco Carrera and Edward Johnson are not to reach Guantanamo. This is a matter of national security. Clearance level red. This conversation never happened.'

You could hear the grind of Craig's molars. 'On whose authority?'

'Above your paygrade. You'll be protected.'

'Protected?' he spat. 'They're shackled, locked down, and in my custody. This isn't protocol—it's an execution.'

'It's justice. Do your job, Lieutenant Ryan.'

The line went dead.

Craig stared at the receiver. For a long moment, he didn't move. Didn't breathe.

Back in the cabin, Alessandro looked up as Craig returned, pale and grim.

'Everything okay?' he asked, sensing the shift in the air.

Craig didn't answer right away. He glanced toward Marco and Eddie—still cuffed, still silent. Still alive.

Then he looked back at Alessandro.

'Not even close.'

Rumours had spread that Champaign PD, Steelvale officials, and the state governor had struck an unprecedented deal with the Feds. They weren't taking any more chances; Marco and Eddie had to be stopped in their tracks. And Guantanamo Bay was the only solution. Period. *So, why that call?* Craig thought.

The flight buzzed with a pressure no altitude could explain. Craig didn't speak. He barely blinked. Every sound—the hum of the engine, the click of seat buckles, the rustle of fabric—felt louder somehow. The weight of that voice, that order, sat on his chest like a cinder block.

He replayed the call over and over in his mind. No names. No signatures. No protocol. Just a shadow directive from someone high enough to pull the strings—and expect him to be the blade. But Craig wasn't a hitman. And he sure as hell wasn't a pawn. So he did the only thing he could.

He said nothing, and let the flight continue.

Approximately two hours later, Craig returned from the cockpit, frowning. 'We just picked up a scrambled signal. Someone tried pinging the jet—encrypted burst. Pilot's rerouting.'

Alessandro shot him a look. 'Pinged how?'

'External satellite link. Someone knows we've got them in the air, and is determined to either terminate them or save them. Not sure which.'

Eddie sat up straighter. 'Told you. We've got friends.'

Stepping forward, Craig backhanded the smirk off him. 'Your friends are next. If this is some kind of mid-air rescue plan, you'd better hope they brought wings and parachutes.'

A shudder passed through the plane. Everyone tensed.

The pilot's voice crackled through the intercom. 'We've got a drone following us. Not armed. Possibly just surveillance. We're climbing to avoid detection.'

Craig and Alessandro exchanged a glance. Marco's smile returned—slow and chilling.

'You can land this plane, Craig,' he said. 'Or you can crash it. Either way, they're coming.'

Craig stormed forward, leaned in close to him, and said coldly, 'Let them. I'll drag you out of the wreckage myself and still make sure you get to Cuba breathing just enough for them to finish you off.'

When the plane touched down on Cuban soil, the skies were dark. A blacked-out convoy waited on the tarmac. Razor wire glittered in the spotlights beyond the chain-link perimeter.

Marco stepped off the plane, surrounded by armed guards. The air was hot and suffocating.

Eddie blinked at the guards, rattled for the first time. 'Where...

where are we?'

Craig gave him a grin. 'Welcome to paradise.'

As the two fugitives were hauled toward the concrete entrance of the compound, Marco turned his head one last time. 'You'll never break me.'

'That's the thing,' Craig said. 'I don't need to. This place will do it for me.'

Marco's mouth curled into something between a smile and a snarl.

'Checkmate,' he whispered.

Craig froze.

Alessandro muttered, 'You hear that?'

'Yeah,' Craig said, his jaw tightening. 'The game's not over.'

<h1 style="text-align:center">CHAPTER 32
THE GATES OF HELL</h1>

The infamous fortress loomed over them, surrounded by razor wire, guard towers, and armed soldiers. This wasn't just any prison; this was Guantanamo Bay—the end of the line for men like them.

Marco's eyes burned with a mixture of defiance and fear. He stared hard at Eddie, trying to will him into understanding, to apply that telepathic bond they used to joke about. Eddie glanced back at him, his face a mask of resignation. He gave a slow shrug, his shoulders heavy with the weight of surrender. It was over. They both knew it. No more escape plans. No more clever tricks. They were at Guantanamo Bay now, and this was where hope came to die.

Craig walked behind them, eyes darting from guard to guard, still rattled. He didn't trust a single soul now. Not the soldiers. Not the officials. Not even Alessandro. And certainly not Marco Carrera.

Someone had wanted those men dead before they ever stepped off the plane. And that meant someone was still pulling strings in the dark.

He wasn't done yet.

The heavy steel gates groaned as they swung open, and Marco felt a chill run down his spine. The place had an aura of suffocating dread, the kind of dread that broke men—whether they were guilty or not. The guards weren't your average prison guards, either.

These were soldiers, military-trained, stone-faced, and armed to the teeth. There was no room for rebellion here. No cracks to slip through.

'This place is a fortress,' Marco muttered under his breath.

Eddie didn't respond, but his eyes told Marco everything—there was no way out of here. Not this time.

As they marched inside, they got glimpses of the detention centre's layout. It was built like a nightmare come to life. Stark concrete walls, razor-wire fences, and guard towers that seemed to watch every inch of the prison. The cells were small, dark, and barely big enough for a man to stretch his arms.

A large, imposing figure with a sneer etched across his face approached them as they were led through the yard.

'Welcome to hell, boys,' the guard grunted. 'You think you're tough? You ain't seen nothin' yet. We *will* break you.'

Marco felt the man's eyes on him, burning with cold contempt. He kept his mouth shut, though anger bubbled beneath the surface. He had been in tough spots before, but this... this was different. The very air of the place seemed designed to crush your spirit.

Inside the prison, the smell of damp concrete and disinfectant filled their noses. Fluorescent lights buzzed overhead, casting a sickly green glow over everything. They were taken down a long corridor, each footstep echoing off the walls. The guards didn't say much—just shoved them forward with the cold efficiency of men who had done this a thousand times before.

They were thrust into a cold room at the end of the corridor with metal chairs bolted to the floor. An officer sat behind the desk, eyes cold and calculating.

'This isn't Steelvale,' the officer said. 'You try anything here— anything at all—and you'll wish you never had. There are no second chances. No mercy. You're not just inmates here; you're prisoners of war. And we don't play nicely with enemies.'

Marco swallowed fury, jaw rigid. He glanced at Eddie, who stared blankly ahead, shoulders slumped.

'You'll be put in solitary for now,' the officer continued. 'That'll give you time to reflect on how far you've fallen. After that, you'll be processed. But don't get too comfortable—this place has a way of making time crawl.'

The guards dragged them toward solitary. Doors slammed, and darkness swallowed them.

CHAPTER 33
DEAD MEN WALKING

Hours passed. Marco sat in the silence of his cramped cell, fury simmering beneath his skin, gut churning with rage, fear and regret. How had it come to this? They'd been so close to freedom, to disappearing into the shadows of London. And now here they were, locked in the most notorious prison in the world.

A tray scraped through a slot in the door. He picked at the food, barely noticing the taste. Not enough to survive on. Just enough to stay conscious.

Then—footsteps. A guard entered.

'You're being moved.'

Marco tensed. Eddie, mute in the next cell, stirred.

They were marched to another block. A larger cell. One man already inside. Standing in the shadows, back turned.

A whisper, flat and ghostly:

'You'll never get out.'

Marco froze. It was familiar. Too familiar.

He stared hard at the figure in the shadows.

Recognition hit like a thunderclap.

'So, where did we leave off?' The words, louder now, sliced through the stagnant air like a scalpel through old flesh, each syllable deliberate, dripping with malice. 'Was it three days?'

Marco's pulse stuttered. That voice—precise, venomous, almost intimate—filled the cellblock with a quiet, creeping dread. It was the voice of a man who'd once whispered secrets to the dark. It was the voice that had silenced Surly. And now it was back for more.

Slowly, the man turned.

Marco hadn't seen X since Steelvale. Not since the night the fire lit the sky and the walls came down. Not since Surly screamed into oblivion and Marco was left with nothing but Rip—the last piece, the worst piece. The only piece that ever truly understood his rage.

Now... now that, too, was in danger.

From the beginning, Marco had known that his pretence at friendship was just that: a pretence. Marco had played along with it, indulged it, waiting to find out what X's angle was—and, deep down, he'd been grateful for the break from that relentless torment.

But here, finally, playtime was over. And X stood in the shadows like a nightmare given bones.

'I asked you a question.' X's cold, calculating tone slithered into Marco's ears, radiating a chill that even Guantanamo's concrete couldn't block, his smile curled across his face like a scar splitting open. 'Was it three days? Or was it four? I lose track. Time's funny when you're rotting in a cage.'

'What the hell are you doing here?' Marco growled. His fists were already clenched. Not out of fear—not yet. Out of instinct.

X laughed. Low and sick.

'Oh, Marco. You haven't changed. Always so dramatic. So eager to throw a punch. So desperate to prove you're still in control. You're not, by the way. Just thought I'd let you in on that little secret.'

Eddie shifted beside Marco, his breath shallow, eyebrows knitting in confusion.

'This isn't right,' he whispered.

X wasn't supposed to be here. Not in this timeline. Not in this dimension.

'Why do you think I'm really here?' He leaned toward Marco, his breath like acid, then released another bitter laugh. 'You fucking idiot! I did it to get close to you. To finish what you and I started. To settle our unfinished business.' As X went on, his voice lilted with theatrical glee. 'Oh, before I forget. Your little man, Giles? He squealed. Sold your soul to save his own skin. But alas, he got a knife in the neck for his troubles. And look at me—I'm still standing.'

Marco's eyes narrowed. 'What are you going on about?'

X stepped forward, close enough now that Marco could see the veins pulsing in his neck, the fire flickering in those dead eyes.

'I'm here because I chose to be. I'm here to kill Rip.'

Silence.

Then Marco's voice cracked, not with fear—but something far worse.

'You can't.'

'Oh, but I can,' X whispered, almost lovingly. 'See, Surly was easy. A blunt object. A fool with fists. But Rip? Rip is clever. Rip is cruel. Rip is... you, without the mask. That's what makes this fun.'

Muscles twitched along Marco's jaw. 'Rip is who I became when the world stopped playing fair.'

'Rip,' X said softly, 'is who you became when you realized you were nothing by yourself.'

Marco lunged—rage blind, fury raw—but X was ready. He didn't move. Just raised one hand. Not to block. Not to fight. To stop time. And as if he really had some kind of supernatural power, Marco found himself freezing still. Eddie watched on, pressed back against the cell's wall, eyes wide and unblinking.

'Rip is your illusion,' X whispered. 'And I've come to unmake him.'

He leaned in close, staring into Marco's soul.

'Tell me... what does Rip fear the most?'

Marco's chest heaved. 'Nothing.'

'Wrong,' X said gently. 'Rip fears exposure. Truth. The mirror that shows him as a boy lost in the fog, pretending to be a god.'

And then X started reciting.

It wasn't a chant. It wasn't a spell. It was worse—it was the truth.

Line by line, he dismantled every lie Rip had ever told. He spoke of Marco, of the child he had once been. Of the night when he was admonished by a priest as an altar boy. Of the rivers of blood he unleashed in revenge, and of the deals made in whispers. He dragged every buried secret into the light, until Rip—inside Marco's mind—started to scream.

'No,' Marco whispered, staggering back. 'No, no, stop—he's not—'

'Oh, he is,' X hissed. 'He's pathetic. He's desperate. And most of all—he's gone.'

Marco fell to his knees, fists in his hair. The scream that tore from his throat wasn't human. It was Rip's final gasp. A death rattle inside the mind of a man unravelling.

X knelt beside him. 'Now you're free,' he murmured. 'No more alter egos. No more delusions. Just you.'

He stood, brushing imaginary dust from Marco's jacket.

'And you, Marco Carrera? You're nothing without Rip. Just another broken soul waiting to be devoured.'

And with that, X walked away. Not in triumph. Not in anger. But with the calm, quiet certainty of a man who had finally finished the masterpiece he'd been carving for years. The barred door buzzed open for him, and clanged shut in his wake.

The cellblock was quiet now. Too quiet.

X's footsteps faded into the distance, each echo a hammer blow in Marco's skull. He remained on his knees, breath ragged, staring at nothing. The air felt hollow, weighted by Rip's absence—his voice, his venom, his dark comfort. Gone.

Eddie reached out cautiously.

'Marco...?'

His voice cracked like glass. He'd never seen Marco like this. Not even after Steelvale. Not even after Surly.

Marco didn't move. Not at first. His lips twitched. His fingers scraped at the concrete floor like he was trying to claw his way into the earth. His body trembled—not from cold, but from the sudden, terrifying emptiness. He opened his mouth to speak, but nothing came out. No wisecrack. No threat. No Rip.

He was alone in there.

And he knew it.

'I don't...' he croaked finally, the words struggling through his throat like rusted gears grinding back to life. 'I don't hear him anymore.'

Eddie knelt beside him. 'Hear who?'

Marco's eyes, bloodshot and wild, turned to him.

'Rip.'

The word landed like a grenade between them.

Eddie stepped back. He'd always known Marco had... pieces. Layers. But this? This was like watching a skyscraper implode in slow motion. Steel bones folding. Foundations crumbling.

'He's gone,' Marco whispered. He pressed his fingers to his temples. 'He's really gone. It's just me in here now.'

'Maybe that's a good thing,' Eddie offered carefully.

Marco laughed. A jagged, humourless sound. 'No. No, it's not. You don't get it. Rip did what I couldn't. Rip kept me alive when the walls closed in. Rip knew how to fight dirty. Rip didn't flinch.

And now...'

He slammed his fists against the floor, once, twice—hard enough to crack skin.

'Now I'm just a hollowed-out shell! Just the scared kid X always said I was!'

Eddie swallowed. 'So... what now?'

Marco looked up, his face a twisted mask of despair and fury.

'I rebuild him.'

Eddie froze. 'What?'

'I bring him back.'

Marco stood slowly, swaying on unsteady legs. His voice dropped to a low, obsessive whisper.

'He's not dead. Not really. X thinks he erased him—but Rip isn't some ghost you can just exorcise. He's in the cracks. In the blood. In every lie I've ever told myself. I just have to dig deep enough.'

Eddie's face turned pale. 'Marco, you're scaring me.'

'You should be scared,' Marco snarled. 'Because if I can't bring Rip back, then I'll become something worse. Something X didn't plan for.'

He took a step forward, eyes blazing now—not with Rip's cold calculation, but with something raw, unstable.

'X thinks he's won. But all he's done is burn the map. Now I have no rules. No conscience. No voice in my head keeping the beast on a leash.'

A pause.

'Rip was the mask,' Marco said softly. 'Now it's just me.'

With that, he turned toward the wall of the cell, staring into it like it held the answer to everything. Planning. Plotting. Breathing. Not quite whole. Not quite human. But alive... somehow.

And whatever was rising from the ashes of Rip... it wasn't done yet.

* * *

Slowly but surely, Guantanamo was stripping Marco down to a shell of his former self. Eyes hollowed from weeks of torment, he sat in the corner of his cell, gaunt and staring.

Eddie, a mere shadow of himself, had stopped eating fourteen days ago. He was wasting away; the hunger strikes were a silent protest, a desperate bid to end the misery on his terms.

X had claimed Marco as his, and the other prisoners knew better than to intervene. Everyone respected the unspoken rules. X moved through the cell block like a predator, locked doors opening for him like magic, always circling Marco, waiting for the right moment to strike again. And today, it seemed, would be that day.

X's eyes, once cold, now blazed with something deeper. Older. Vengeful. As he entered the cell, his movements were calm, as if he were savouring every second of the torment he'd inflicted. Marco's head lifted slowly, his breath laboured yet still defiant.

'Do you think I came to Guantanamo just to kill Rip?'

Marco's jaw twitched. Something in X's tone—serene, unshaken, obsessed—sent a ripple of fear up his spine.

'What are you talking about now, for fuck's sake?' he snapped back. 'I didn't do anything to you.'

X's face twisted into a sneer. 'You never understood, did you, Marco? This was never just about you and me. You don't know what I sacrificed to get to you. But I did it. All of it. For one reason.'

Marco swallowed hard, trying to muster some strength. 'You think you've won? What are you, a puppet? Please. You're nothing.'

The smile dropped from X's face like a guillotine. 'You forgot everything you've done already? How convenient.'

He stepped forward, each footfall echoing like a countdown.

'You. Killed. My. Sister. This is about Ava.'

At the mention of her name, Marco's eyes darkened. He was confused. Ava? X's sister? He knew the pain in X ran deeper than just the usual prison grudges. But before he could speak, X stepped right up to him, crouching down to meet his gaze.

'Let me officially introduce myself to you. My name is Luca. Luca Larsson, Ava's eldest brother.'

The words hit Marco like a steel fist to the gut. The cell seemed to shrink, the air sucked out. He blinked at X—Luca—searching for some sign that this was an exaggeration. A bluff. But the fury in Luca's eyes was no performance.

'Ava was the glue that held our family together,' Luca continued, his voice taut and emotional. 'She was everything to us. My parents? They were hanging on by a thread, but Ava—she made them believe things would be okay, that we had a future.'

Marco looked away, his lips tight, refusing to engage, but Luca wouldn't let him off the hook that easily.

'You took her from us,' Luca spat. 'You didn't just kill her. You killed *all* of us. My parents, they're ghosts now. They barely speak. The life they had, the love they had, all gone. And why? Because you couldn't control yourself. Because you—' He stopped, clenching his fists, fighting to keep control of his rage. 'You destroyed her. You destroyed us.'

Marco's voice was barely a whisper. 'She shouldn't have lied about me.'

Luca's laugh was hollow, bitter. 'You delusional twat. She told the truth, and you know it! It all came out in court. You had no right to kill her, you piece of shit. You just didn't care. You were too wrapped up in your little power games.'

Marco's jaw clenched, but Luca pressed on.

'After Ava, I couldn't function anymore. I couldn't even look at my parents. Therapy didn't work; soon enough, I was down the same road you were on. Crime. Violence. I didn't care about anything. You took everything from me, Marco.'

There was silence for a moment, the weight of the truth pressing down on them both. Then, Luca leaned in, his voice low and dangerous.

'Do you know what it's like to wake up every single night gasping for air because you're haunted by what you did to your family? By the shame you brought on them? Every day, I saw the pain in their eyes, the same pain you caused. You ruined our lives, Marco. But now? It's not all lost. I turned my life around, I became a forensic psychiatrist, and I'm back in my parents' good graces. This time, it's my turn to ruin you.'

Marco's breath hitched as Luca's words sank in. Hearing it out loud—the pure hatred, the loss, the pain—was unbearable.

'I'm getting out of here,' Luca said, straightening up, his expression turning icy again. 'I'll see my parents soon, and we'll enjoy whatever's left of our lives. And you... You'll be rotting in an unmarked grave, forgotten. When they finally pull the plug on you, no one will care. No one will even remember your name.'

Marco forced a laugh, though it came out more like a rasp. 'You really think you'll just walk away from this? Like you didn't sell your soul to get here? They're using you, Luca. They'll throw you out with the rest of the trash when they're done.'

Luca's face twisted into a smile that sent chills through Marco. 'Oh, they've already given me my prize. But alas, you escaped before I could do the honours. So, yes, I was given a free pass. I get to kill you and walk out of here without a single charge. Immunity, in exchange for your head. It's better than winning the fucking lottery.'

Marco's eyes widened in disbelief.

'That's right,' Luca said. He spoke with the slow drag of someone savouring the moment. 'When I'm done with you, I walk. And no one will stop me.'

There was a long pause as Marco stared up at Luca, realization dawning on him. This wasn't just a vendetta. It was orchestrated, a setup from the start.

'The Champaign PD and Steelvale,' Luca began. His eyes gleamed with the ruthless satisfaction of a predator relishing its kill. 'They struck a deal with me. A good one. They planted me in Steelvale and gave me everything I needed to dismantle you piece by piece. In return, I give them you.' He chuckled, the sound sharp enough to cut. 'Yes, Carrera... You. Your mind and body.'

Luca spread his arms, his confidence as unyielding as steel. 'I get to walk out of here when I'm done playing with you. Back to my life.' His gaze hardened, his grin growing even more sinister. 'You see? This was always about Ava.'

Marco's heart raced. He tried to hide the panic rising in his chest, but Luca saw it and revelled in it.

Eddie, who neither of them had realised was even conscious, pushed himself up with wasted, trembling arms. 'Luca, listen— maybe this isn't the place to—'

'Shut your mouth!' Luca turned on him, eyes wild. 'You're just his pet. His little sidekick. You don't know what he's capable of.'

He dragged a breath in through clenched teeth and refocused on Marco.

'You thought you were untouchable. You thought you could get away with everything you did. But look at you now.' His voice lowered to a deadly whisper. 'Your life's measured by a ticking clock, and the time's almost up.'

As Marco clenched his fists, struggling to steady his breathing, he could feel the walls closing in, the end approaching faster than he'd ever anticipated. He opened his mouth, but no words came out. All his old confidence, his schemes, his plans—it all cracked under the weight of Luca's rage.

His voice, when it finally emerged, was thin.

'You think you'll get away with this? You think the guards will let you do whatever the hell you want?'

Luca's laugh was pure poison. 'You still don't get it, do you?' He looked around the dim cell. 'This place isn't for the living, Marco. It's for the forgotten. The disposable. The ones nobody writes letters to, nobody comes for, nobody cares about.'

His eyes bored into Marco.

'And that means... nobody's going to stop me.'

CHAPTER 34
LOCKED AND LOADED

Just as the tension reached its peak, a sharp metallic clang rang out down the corridor. All three men froze.

Click. Clack.

The bolts of the main gate locked into place. The deep snaps echoed like a warning.

Then—

Bang.

Their cell door opened.

They stepped cautiously into the open, dazed, blinking in the low flicker of the corridor lights.

'What the hell's going on?' Eddie whispered, nerves tight as a wire.

Marco shook his head. 'Stay put. Eyes up.'

Luca just grinned, with almost childlike delight. 'Ooh... this is getting interesting.'

From the far end of the corridor, a silhouette emerged. Heavy boots hit the ground like drums of war. The light behind the figure made it hard to see his face. But even in shadow, his presence was unmistakable—massive, authoritative, cold as ice.

Marco's heart dropped into his stomach. 'It's not a guard,' he murmured.

The figure stepped into full view.

And Marco's blood stopped.

Standing there—decked in full military black, face half-shadowed by a cap, eyes hidden behind mirrored shades—was the last person Marco needed to see again. And he wasn't there to stop Luca.

He was there to help.

'So, here we are again,' Craig said, his voice low and steely with authority. 'Face to face. You thought you could play us, taunt us, and keep escaping like you're invincible. But look where you are now.'

Marco and Eddie remained frozen, unable to decipher what was unfolding.

As the door clanged shut behind Craig, the dim light revealed Riaan and Alessandro —heavily armed, expressions hard and unforgiving.

The corner of Craig's mouth curled in condescension. 'Looks like you're in quite the predicament. No human rights groups can help you now. Finally, it's just you and the enhanced interrogation techniques used here without interference. But don't worry. We're here to ensure this ends... one way or another.'

Luca glanced at Craig, then back at Marco. 'Well, well. Looks like today's going to be even more eventful than I thought.'

Marco clenched his fists, but he stayed silent. Eddie shifted beside him, nerves on edge, and didn't dare speak. This wasn't a situation they could talk their way out of.

Alessandro stepped forward, his face expressionless, his eyes dark with intent. 'You've had your chances,' he said quietly. 'But this time, it's different.'

'Different how?' Marco finally spat, unable to contain himself. 'You think locking us in here is gonna break us? We've been through worse.'

Riaan smiled faintly, his eyes like cracked ice. 'Oh, you misunderstand, Carrera. This isn't about breaking you. This is about ending things. Once and for all.'

He and Craig pulled out small black devices from their pockets. Not guns, but something more subtle. More terrifying.

Eddie stepped back, panic starting to edge into his voice. 'What the hell are those?'

'An insurance policy,' Craig replied coolly. 'See, the feds don't want you escaping again. Neither do we. So, we made sure you won't get another chance.'

Marco's mind raced as he tried to figure out what they were up to, but then Craig hit a button on his device. A deafening beep echoed through the block, and the lights flickered once, twice, then went out completely.

Total darkness.

Panic set in, and Marco could hear Eddie breathing hard beside him.

'Marco, what's happening? What did they do?'

A voice rang through the darkness—Craig's, calm and controlled. 'You've been tagged, Carrera. Both of you. Microchips implanted during processing. That beep? It just activated them.'

'What the hell?' Marco's voice trembled for the first time.

Riaan's laugh was low. Sinister. 'Don't bother running. Wherever you go, we'll find you. You're done.'

Marco's pulse pounded in his ears. This couldn't be real. Microchips? He could barely process it. 'You bastards!'

Craig continued, his words drifting like cold smoke down the corridor.

'We're here because some debts need collecting. And tonight... Tonight, we're giving the other prisoners a choice.'

He paused for a long moment, as if savouring the taste of his victory.

'They can deal with you. Or we will.'

Eddie stiffened beside Marco. 'Wait... You're letting them—'

'Yes,' Craig cut in, voice sharp as a blade. 'After what you've done, after all the blood and betrayal, do you really think anyone in this place wants you to walk out alive? Hell, they've been waiting for this moment. You'll be lucky to last ten minutes.'

The unmistakable click of boots echoed in the darkness, followed by a resounding clang as the heavy doors slammed shut once again behind Craig, Alessandro, and Riaan, locking Marco and Eddie inside with the rest of the prisoners.

CHAPTER 35
THE RECKONING

There were no alarms. No shouts. No warnings.

Just the sickening echo of bolts sliding into place—slow, final, deliberate.

Then silence.

Not the peaceful kind. The kind that slithers under your skin and tells you something terrible is about to happen.

A slow, menacing creak echoed through the corridor. The lights buzzed back on, yellow-green and garish.

One by one, cell doors opened.

Not with urgency, but with precision. Like a ritual. Like a final act.

Tension rippled across Marco's jaw as prisoners stepped out—slowly, deliberately. Their features were carved in stone, eyes not curious but hungry. Luca leaned back against the far wall, arms crossed, watching like a man who'd set fire to a building and now waited to admire the flames. His lips curved into a predator's grin.

Marco glanced at him, gut twisting. He wasn't used to being the target. He was used to running the game.

But tonight, the rules had changed.

Marco's defiance faltered as he realized the enormity of the situation. He and Eddie weren't facing guards, rules, or bureaucracy anymore. They were facing the wrath of every inmate in Guantanamo.

'Now you're in a place where no one fears you,' said a voice, rough and low.

A hulking man stepped into view. His nose had been broken more than once. His knuckles looked like they'd been carved out of stone.

'In here,' he said, 'you're the prey.'

Marco's heart beat faster, but his face remained hard. 'This isn't your business,' he growled. 'Back off.'

Another voice joined in—higher, but no less venomous. 'We've all been waiting for you, Carrera. We remember. You put half of us in here. Lied. Cut deals. Left your so-called friends to rot while you snaked your way out.'

Eddie looked at Marco, voice trembling. 'They're serious, man. We need a plan—now.'

'There is no plan,' Marco whispered. 'Just survive.'

The hallway filled with inmates, each more terrifying than the last. Some had scars that told stories. Most carried makeshift weapons—shanks, sharpened spoons, broken mop handles wrapped in tape.

Luca chuckled softly from the shadows. 'This is better than I imagined,' he said. 'All that time in Steelvale, watching you walk around like you were untouchable. But here you are. Just another piece of meat.'

They weren't prisoners anymore. They were gladiators.

And the wolves had been unleashed.

The first man lunged. Marco barely dodged him, driving an elbow into his throat. He staggered, coughing violently. Another rushed Eddie, who swung a fist and caught him clean across the jaw—but two more followed. Marco slammed one man's head into the cell bars. Blood burst from his own nose when someone cracked him from behind with a lunch tray.

Chaos ignited like a wildfire. This wasn't Craig, Alessandro, or Riaan's fight anymore. The inmates had taken over, and Marco and Eddie were drowning in the very violence they had unleashed for years.

The cell block became a vortex of fists, fury, and vengeance. Blood sprayed the concrete. Grunts and screams echoed like sounds from an animal pit. Every inch of Marco's body howled with the pain of impact—ribs bruised, face swelling, hands slick with blood.

Eddie was dragged to the floor, kicked viciously. He let out a cry as someone drove a knee into his chest. Marco reached for him, but a pair of hands yanked him away. A prisoner with a long, jagged scar running from cheek to ear smashed him back against the wall, pushing in until they were nose to nose.

'You made enemies everywhere you went, Carrera,' the man hissed, his breath foul with hate. 'Every back you and Noctis stabbed, every so-called friend you sold out, they're all watching now.'

He spat in Marco's face. Marco shoved him off, landing a blow to his gut, but knew it didn't matter.

There were too many. And no help was coming.

Just as a sharpened toothbrush came swinging toward Marco's throat—

BEEEEEEEP!

A shrill alarm blared overhead. Floodlights blazed to life, blinding, white-hot. Boots thundered against the floor like a stampede.

'DOWN! ON YOUR KNEES! HANDS ON YOUR HEAD!'

The inmates scattered, most dropping to the ground, cursing. Craig walked back in, this time flanked by a dozen armed guards.

His face showed no regret. No urgency. No surprise. Just... grim satisfaction. He paced over to where Marco and Eddie lay—wounded, gasping, dazed—and crouched down, face inches from Marco's.

'That,' he whispered, 'was mercy.'

Marco blinked blood from his eyes. 'You... you let them—'

'Yes,' Craig said. 'And I'll do it again.' He stood. 'Get them out of my sight.'

The guards dragged Marco and Eddie back into their cell, slamming the door shut with a force that rattled their bones. Outside, the inmates howled with rage, denied their kill. But the hunger would remain.

Craig turned back, locking eyes with Marco one last time.

'This is just the beginning,' he said softly. 'Sleep well.'

And then he was gone.

The lights dimmed. Darkness crept back in. Marco collapsed against the wall, spitting blood.

Eddie coughed, holding his side. 'We're not getting out of here.'

Marco said nothing. He didn't need to. He just stared at the ceiling, bruised, broken, and seething. Then, through a cracked lip, he muttered, 'Next time... I'll kill every last one of them.'

And the silence of the cell whispered back to him.

CHAPTER 36
COUNTDOWN TO EXECUTION

Guantanamo's air clung like a second skin — hot, dense, and brimming with unspoken menace. Like it had soaked up every scream, every secret, every slow death that had taken place inside its walls. Marco sat on the edge of his bunk, eyes burning holes through the floor, mind grinding through every detail like a machine refusing to jam.

Eddie hadn't moved in hours. He lay on his back as if he were a corpse waiting to be tagged, his eyes vacant, lips slack, hands limp. He wasn't sleeping—he was surrendering. The countdown had started the day they'd arrived. The only thing left was the final click of the clock.

Then came the footsteps.

Boots. Measured, deliberate, merciless. They echoed off the concrete like gunfire, and Clanwell appeared with two guards flanking her like hounds. She stopped in front of the cell, calm and crisp, giving Marco a vulture-eyed look that said she'd been waiting for this moment since the day they met.

'Well, well,' Clanwell said, voice cool as steel. 'I've got good news. You won't have to rot here much longer.'

Marco didn't flinch. 'Cut the theatrics, Clanwell. You came here for a reason. Spit it out.'

Clanwell's smile was tight. 'You're done, Carrera. I put in the request. It's been approved. One month—then it's curtains for you.

Both of you. Clock's ticking.'

Eddie didn't even blink. But Marco stood slowly, like a man pulling his fury up from the soles of his feet. He prowled to the bars and stared Clanwell down.

'You think a date on a piece of paper scares me?' he said quietly. 'You think you can break me with a fucking deadline?'

'I think you broke yourself long ago,' Clanwell said. 'I'm just here to clean up the mess.'

'You're not cleaning up anything. You're just playing executioner because someone finally gave you a sharp stick and told you to poke the lion.'

Clanwell rumbled with dark amusement, filled with venom. 'You always did think you were above it all. But let me remind you—this is Guantanamo. There's no back door, no bribes, no last-minute helicopter ride out. You die here. Dirty. Forgotten. Alone.'

Marco's bloodstained hands gripped the bars. 'You've got no idea who you're dealing with.'

'No?' Clanwell leaned in. 'I know exactly who you are. A washed-up bastard who burned every bridge he ever crossed. Your name's worth jack shit now. Your allies? Gone. Your enemies? Lining up like it's feeding time. Hell, you should be thanking me—I'm giving you a cleaner death than the others would.'

Marco spat on the ground. 'You don't get the last word, Clanwell. Not here. Not ever.'

'You already gave it up the day you crossed me.' Clanwell turned away, but not before tossing a look toward Eddie. 'He's already dead. You just haven't realized it yet.'

As the guards followed Clanwell down the hall, Marco muttered, 'Fucking coward.'

Night fell. The lights dimmed to a sickly mustard glow. Fingers of shadow stretched, gripping every surface. Marco paced the cell like a caged animal. Eddie hadn't moved.

'You just gonna lie there?' Marco barked. 'We're not finished yet.'

Eddie blinked slowly, voice barely audible. 'We've been finished for months.'

'No.' Marco's voice rose, desperate, angry. 'You can't check out now. Not when I still have a way—'

'There is no way,' Eddie cut in flatly. 'There's just a date and a hole in the ground.'

And then, a voice from the darkness.

'I wouldn't be so sure.'

Marco stilled.

From the far side of the corridor, Luca stepped into the light—half-smile etched on his face, arms folded like a man watching the first sparks catch on dry tinder.

'Nice effort, Marco,' Luca said casually. 'Too bad none of it matters anymore.'

Marco stared at him. 'You've been listening this whole time?'

Luca chuckled. 'Oh, I've been doing more than listening. I've been waiting.'

'For what?' Marco asked, eyes narrowed.

'For this moment,' Luca said, stepping closer, expression twisting into something darker. 'When the mighty Marco Carrera realizes that for once... he has no control.'

Marco's fists clenched. 'You got something to say, say it.'

Luca leaned against the cell door, his voice low, intimate. 'I asked to be in this snake pit. You know why?'

Marco didn't answer. His silence was dangerous.

'Because I want to watch you die,' Luca whispered. 'Up close. I want to see your face when the world stops spinning and you finally realize—you lost.'

Marco moved fast, grabbed Luca by the collar, but he didn't flinch.

'You think I'm afraid of you?' he asked. 'You think this is fear? No, Marco. This is justice. Cold. Pure. Unrelenting.'

Eddie sat up, confused, hollow-eyed. 'What the hell is going on?'

Luca turned to him. 'Oh, Eddie. Sweet, useless Eddie. You're just collateral. This was never about you.'

Marco shoved Luca back. 'What are you planning?'

Luca's smile widened. 'You might die in thirty days. Or you might not. That's just what the paperwork says. I've been given... liberties. I can make every second of your life between now and then a living hell. And then maybe, if I'm satisfied, I'll let them flip the switch.'

Marco's chest tightened. 'They'd never let you—'

'They already have.' Luca tapped the metal door with a fingertip. 'This place isn't run by laws anymore. It's run by resentment. Revenge. And me.' His voice dropped to a hiss. 'Every minute you breathe, I'll be there. In the dark. In your dreams. In your nightmares. You'll pray for the end.'

Marco was silent. Still. But his mind was spinning, faster than ever before.

Luca gave a mock salute. 'Sweet dreams, Carrera. They're the only mercy you'll get.'

He backed into the shadows, leaving Marco staring into the void. The silence returned—but it was a different kind of silence now.

And Marco knew the countdown had begun again. But not to death.

To vengeance.

CHAPTER 37
THE FINAL BLOW

Marco had been reduced to an ember of his former fire. Gone was the sharp-tongued tactician, the escape artist who'd laughed in the face of wardens and plotted his way out of every cell they'd ever thrown him in. Now, he crouched in his cage, knees hugged to his chest like a child, his body skeletal, his eyes empty, haunted pits.

Eddie was gone. Starved himself into silence. Twenty-one days without a crumb. A quiet protest; a final act of control in a place where nothing belonged to you—not your body, not your breath, not even your soul. His corpse still lay in the corner of their cell, stiff and stinking. The other prisoners watched Marco from the shadows, silent sentinels who would never touch him again.

Because Marco belonged to Luca. And Luca had plans.

He moved through the cell block like the grim reaper dressed in orange, slow, deliberate, eyes glinting with cold calculation. Today... was the day.

Marco's head lifted. He heard Luca coming before he saw him. The footsteps. That slight drag of the left heel. The sound of hell approaching.

'You ready to finish this?' Luca's voice rang low, deadly calm.

Marco forced himself upright. Every joint screamed. His jaw was split, his ribs cracked from Luca's last beating, but somehow, some shred of the old defiance clawed its way up his throat.

'You're late,' he rasped.

Luca stepped in front of his cell, lips twitching at the corners. 'I wanted to make sure you'd be awake for this.'

With a serpentine whisper, the door eased open.

They circled each other like two wolves with nothing left to lose.

The first blow came fast—Luca's knuckles connecting with Marco's cheekbone in a crack that echoed across the block. Marco stumbled but didn't fall. Blood spilled from his mouth.

'That's for Ava,' Luca hissed.

He hit him again. And again. Marco's legs gave out. He collapsed against the wall, panting, spitting red onto the concrete.

'You think this makes you a hero?' Marco coughed. 'You think she'd want this?'

Luca's voice trembled, raw and full of fury. 'She'd want justice. This is all I have left to give.'

Marco gave a wet, painful chuckle. 'Then you've got nothing.'

Luca lost it. He lunged, raining fists, rage exploding in every swing. And still, Marco smiled through the blood.

'Come on,' Marco whispered. 'Do it. Finish it. Be the monster they said I was.'

And with one final blow of Luca's fist—a right hook charged with years of grief, guilt, and vengeance—Marco collapsed, his head hitting the concrete with a sickening crack.

Still... Silent... Gone.

Luca stood over him, heaving, broken.

The entire world seemed to go quiet.

Luca dropped to his knees beside the body, his voice barely a whisper. 'This is for you, Ava... and you, Mom and Dad. I know I've done terrible things. I've walked through hell, but maybe—just maybe—this will let me crawl out of it.'

Tears streaked down his face. Real ones. Human ones.

'I'm sorry,' he whispered. 'But I had to make it right.'

He sat there for a long time, staring at the ruin before him. Then, slowly, he stood. Shoulders squared. Eyes red, but clear.

He walked out of the cell without looking back.

* * *

Later that night, halfway across the world, the news broke.

MARCO CARRERA DEAD AT GUANTANAMO BAY.

Champaign erupted.

In a private room downtown, Craig read the headline aloud, his jaw slack with disbelief. 'It's real,' he said, breathless. 'The bastard's gone.'

Alessandro laughed—really laughed—for the first time in years. 'Should've been me who took him out,' he said, wiping a tear from his cheek. 'But damn, I'll take it. Gabriella finally has peace.'

Kirsten was already on her phone, fingers flying. 'This is it. My lead story. 'The Devil Dies Behind Bars.' Tomorrow morning's front page.'

And in homes across the city, families held each other tight. The man who'd haunted them was no more. Closure had finally come. Justice, in its bloodiest form, had prevailed.

That was the story they clung to... Until it turned on them.

Back in Guantanamo, Luca sat in the guards' office, staring at the ceiling.

A knock at the door startled him. A guard stepped inside, flanked by a military officer in full uniform. He held a sealed envelope marked TOP SECRET.

'Luca Larsson,' the officer said. 'We need to talk.'

Luca frowned. 'About what?'

The guard passed him the envelope. 'About Carrera.'

Luca stared at the envelope. Hesitated. Then ripped it open.

He scanned the single sheet of paper. And froze.

'No,' he whispered.

The officer's face was grave. 'We need you to prepare yourself.'

Luca looked up slowly, his face pale, lips trembling.

'...His body never made it to the morgue.'

A beat of silence. Then the lights in the prison flickered—once, twice—and cut out.

Blackout.

Somewhere in the darkness, a single scream echoed down the corridor.

CHAPTER 38
ASHES TO ASHES

The van was supposed to make a routine drive from Guantanamo's gates to the helipad, destination, federal crematorium in Florida. No ceremony, no coffin, no name etched on a stone—just fire and forgotten ashes. That was the government's plan. Clean. Efficient. Erased.

But that's not what happened.

Somewhere on the 7 kilometre drive under the veil of a moonless night, two blacked-out SUVs boxed the prison van in near a desolate rest stop. The driver barely had time to blink before floodlights flashed in his rearview mirror, and masked men descended on the van like phantoms.

'Federal transport. Step out,' a voice ordered through a voice scrambler.

'But—'

The driver and the guard escorting him were hauled out, gagged, and zip-tied. No shots fired. No blood spilled. Just silence, precision, and dread. By the time the prison officials realized the van had gone dark, the body was already gone.

Noctis had spoken. And The Architect was behind it.

The funeral was not publicized, but word still spread like wildfire in underground circles—Marco Carrera, the infamous creator of carnage, was getting a burial fit for a kingpin. The Architect arranged it in a remote Sicilian graveyard with blood ties and ancient oaths woven into its soil.

High-ranking Noctis members flew in by private jet. Old allies, former enemies, crooked politicians, and merciless mercenaries gathered like shadows among the olive trees. They didn't come to mourn. They came to mark the moment.

The Architect stood at the head of the grave, draped in a tailored black suit, a single red rose in his gloved hand, his face hidden behind a featureless mask. The casket gleamed midnight black with brushed steel accents, a coffin suitable for a fallen emperor. There were no hymns, no dirges, just silence, broken only by the rustling wind and the heavy thud of earth being shovelled aside.

'He was a bastard,' The Architect finally said, addressing the crowd. 'But he was our bastard. He made his mark on this world—love it or hate it—and I'll be damned if I let the government torch him like trash.'

A murmur of agreement.

'I didn't do this for Marco,' he added, voice lower now. 'I did it for Noctis. For our legacy. Men like him... they burn too bright to be extinguished by paperwork.'

As the coffin was lowered, the crowd bowed their heads. And that's when it happened.

Crack!

The single shot rang out like a lightning bolt tearing through heaven.

Chaos erupted. Men ducked. Guns were drawn. The Architect stumbled back, clutching his side—blood blooming against his shirt.

'Sniper!' someone shouted.

But there was no sniper.

Amid the crowd, two mourners blended into the bedlam. One older, slightly hunched with dark sunglasses and a cane. The other younger, clean-shaven. Both wore black hats pulled low.

No one recognized them. But the glint of cold metal peeking from beneath their coats said everything.

The Architect collapsed to his knees, gasping. He looked up, scanning the crowd with unfocused eyes. 'Cowards... all of you...'

No one came forward. The shooter had vanished into the sea of mourners, and everyone inhaled suspicion with every breath.

Leaning on his prop cane, Craig turned slightly toward Alessandro. 'You notice how he flinched before the shot?' he murmured.

Alessandro nodded. 'He knew it was coming.'

Craig's eyes hardened behind his sunglasses. 'Then it wasn't justice. It was mercy.'

They walked away without a word, fading into the dusk, their silhouettes swallowed by the hills.

The Architect bled out beside the grave of the man he revered. The Cabal—fractured and stunned—watched silently. No one helped. No one spoke. They knew what this meant.

It was over.

The era of Marco Carrera had ended with the bang of a bullet buried inside the man who fed his fire. The evil that plagued Champaign had been cauterized at its roots—not by law, not by war, but by two men who knew what the cost of silence truly was.

As the sun dipped beneath the hills and the grave was filled, the world moved on.

But legends linger.

And in the darkest corners of memory, in Isabella's eyes when she looked at Alessandro, in Kirsten's mind when she studied Craig, the question still whispered:

Who pulled the trigger?

EPILOGUE: THE SILENCE AFTER

The real story died with The Architect. But the truth was far more twisted.

Three months later, a cold rain fell on downtown Chicago. A woman sat at a café window, sipping an espresso, scanning a manila folder full of photos, names, and transcripts that had no business being public.

One image was circled in red: Zeb Landon. Alias—'The Architect'. Deceased.

Another: Ramon Martinez. Alias—'Marco Carrera'. Presumed deceased. No body recovered.

Kirsten closed the folder slowly, slid it into her bag, and tapped a small recording device in her coat pocket. 'Operation Black Veil. Phase One complete. Targets neutralized. But... a deeper rot remains.'

Outside, the city bustled.

Unaware.

Unbothered.

But somewhere beneath the surface, echoes stirred.

In a prison yard in Northern Italy, a wiry inmate paused mid-run, his eyes catching the faint shadow of a raven perched on the wall. His lip curled. 'Took them long enough.'

Travelli—betrayed, abandoned, and locked away for life—despised Marco with a passion and without a shred of apology.

His cousin. His so-called 'family.' Revenge wasn't a thought—it was his purpose.

To him, Marco wasn't just a criminal; he was a contagion—a poison that seeped through the underworld and destroyed, crossing oceans and borders from Naples to Bogotá, from Montreal to Marrakesh. And he welcomed the reckoning.

The raven twitched. Travelli didn't blink. 'Burn in hell, Marco,' he muttered.

Luca hadn't stopped—not until he avenged Ava. He'd sold his soul in the process, crossed lines he could never uncross. But he had no regrets. He did what had to be done to secure the justice his family so rightfully deserved. Now, at last, he was at peace and settled—quietly rebuilding a life in Mauritius, far from the shadows he'd left behind.

In a quiet corner of Sanremo, beyond the reach of the chaos they'd outlasted, Alessandro slid the final round into the box. A faint smile touched his lips. His voice, low but sure, carried the weight of victory. 'We did it our way.'

Waves hammered the shore. Inside the Nantucket beach house, Craig snapped the leather-bound journal shut and dropped it onto the table.

'That bastard,' he muttered. 'That miserable, manipulative bastard... never stopped burning.'

He turned to the window. Sunset flared across the glass, splitting his reflection down the middle. A beat. Then, barely audible—**'Maybe I lit the match.'**

A gunshot echoed—Not now, from memory.

Craig didn't flinch.

Outside, the tide dragged a blackened log back into the sea.

Because some legacies don't die, they harden.

Noctis may have fallen. The empire may have crumbled. But the scars of Marco Carrera's reign remained etched into the concrete of every city he touched.

Some called it justice. Others, vengeance.

But those who truly knew...

Those who bore the weight of truth...

They called it a reckoning.

And in that silence after all the chaos, a single thought remained:

Evil doesn't disappear. It just changes its name.

T H E   E N D